ALSO BY DYLAN

Series

The Blood Rite Saga

The Blood Empire: Episode One

The Blood Princess: Episode One

The Blood Princess: Episode Two

The Blood Princess: Episode Three

The Blood Princess: Episode Four

The Chronicles of Gandos

The Sword of Light

The Aurora Chronicles

Child of Winter

Lake of Prophecy

Britney Allen: The London Crime Syndicate

Blood of Babes: The Slasher Files

Standalone

Lost in Space

The Lone Survivor

Mr. Buddy Bot

Evelyn

For information contact : purplepress.org

First Edition: March 2017

I dedicate this book to my friends and family who have always supported in my dream of being a professional author.

— DYLAN KEEFER

Episode One

THE BLOOD PRINCESS

The Blood Rite Saga

USA Today Bestselling Author

DYLAN KEEFER

CHAPTER ONE

Her heart was beating so fast she thought it was going to jump out of her chest. Flashes of brick walls and floorboards mixed with the blind spots in her vision. She struggled to move her limp body across the bloody wooden floor. The stench of death loomed over her. The pain in her broken legs shot up her body like electricity every time she moved. Her surroundings were blurry. The spots were getting bigger. There was tightness in her chest. A figure stood over her and stretched out a hand. She screamed.

Her eyes opened, and her body involuntarily shot up. She hit her head almost immediately. She was shoved back down from the impact, hitting the back of her head. She opened her eyes. Darkness was all she could see, and pain spread around her skull. She was lightheaded. The air around her was heavy and thick when she inhaled. It made her feel like she was suffocating. She tried to push whatever was on top of her out of the way. When she put her hands in front of her, all she felt was stone. She checked all around her, touching the walls on both sides and the one she was laying on. She was trapped, lying in a stone prison.

She started slamming her fists against the stone on top of her. Her hoarse voice ripped out of her throat, causing her pain. She screamed for help until her throat felt like it was filled with broken glass. She couldn't breathe. Her whole body shook. She needed to get out of there. There was no air, no light, no nothing. A faint cracking noise sounded. Her hand rammed through the stone, breaking it into a thousand pieces.

A gust of air shoved its way in. It calmed her a little. Only faint light streamed down from the medium sized hole at around head level. She reached up, breaking the cracked pieces of stone around the hole, worming her way out. The light was blinding.

She inhaled as deep as she could despite the fact the air felt like ice shards stabbing her lungs. She was afraid it was going to escape from her again. Scrambling out of the stone box she sat down on the floor, hugging her knees to her chest, shivering. Her mind was swirling around and around. When she closed her eyes all she could see were the bloody floorboards and the shadowy figure.

She sat there, rocking back and forth until she was no longer shaking, and her breath was steady. Her eyes were now somewhat used to the light, and the only thing that hurt was her slowly swelling hand. She looked around.

The structure she was in was a completely gray cube made of stone, aside from the wooden door. There were two stained glass windows. Each had a different colorful bird with large wings on it. They were on opposite sides of each other, right in the middle of the long walls. She got up and turned, almost falling down from what she saw.

There were several stone coffins on slabs all around. She was in a mausoleum. She looked down to the one she had burst from. The lid was in pieces, as well some of the sides. But the first name was still legible. Prudence.

No, no, no. I'm not dead. She felt her heart speed up again. She was out of breath as flashes of a knife holding hand filled her mind. Then she was back on that floor, heart in her throat, desperately trying to get away. Need to get out. Need to run.

She scrambled, running backward, and soon tripped over the dress she wore. She hit the wooden door with her back. Before she could regain her balance, the hinges gave away, and she fell with the door.

The impact shook her to the core, and the bright light felt like scalding water pouring over her bare arms. She got up, surprised she had that much strength. Around her were other stone houses like the one she came out of. There were also round marble slabs all around her, with different names and ages on them. She realized she was in a graveyard. Rows of tall trees framed the graves. Their branches hung over the memorials, producing a thick shade all around.

She couldn't stay in the sun anymore, it was blurring her vision, and her skin felt sore. She walked over to the closest tree to hide under its shade. Her body was a burden to her, the pain in her arms and back spreading over her, pushing her down into the earth. The muscles in her body were rigid. She did all she could to push the nightmare away from her mind for now. But the images sprouted up like mushrooms, haunting her.

To ignore them, she focused on remembering the name she saw on the coffin she came out of. Prudence. She couldn't remember if that was her name or not. In fact, she realized she couldn't remember anything about her life. Apart from the nightmare. She clutched onto that name, hoping it was hers.

Prudence was rubbing her now bruised and swollen hand, staring at the short grass. She noticed a curious shadow. It was longer than all the branches and was swinging back and forth in the wind. The shape reminded her of something…

CHAPTER TWO

A sharp pain, as if a knitting needle was boring into her mind crumpled her to the ground. The world around her melted away and she was pushing through a crowd. Prudence's hand was not swollen. It was gripping a shawl wrapped around her head instead. A mixture of smells and voices filled her mind. The torches around her made her flinch. She pushed her way through the crowd until she was far enough to see what was going on.

A woman stood on a wooden stage with a rope around her neck. Her hair was wet and matted. Her eyes were red, and her face was swollen. Her frail, malnourished body was shivering in the wind. The man next to her pushed her over, and she fell down, closing her eyes. A crack echoed, followed by cheering.

The image faded and muddled with Prudence's surroundings. Her breath stuck in her throat. She couldn't stop seeing the woman's face no matter how much she shook her head.

Prudence got up and started running. As if getting away from that spot would also mean getting away from those nightmares. She didn't care if the sun was shining on her, or if the stones she tripped on left bruises and cuts on her legs. After a while, she didn't even feel the ground under her feet.

When she finally tripped hard enough on a root, she didn't hit the ground. She flew out of the graveyard, and her body collided with something metal traveling at a great speed. Her bones cracked under pressure. The force warped her body in front of her very eyes. The metal stopped, and Prudence flew out, hitting the ground.

"Oh, fuck!" A rough male voice reached Prudence's ears.

She opened her eyes, the massive pain radiating from every part of her body was the only thing she could think of. She saw her arm. That is not how an arm should bend was the only thing she could think of. The man above her was panicking.

"Okay okay, you're alive. Hold on, please. Come on you goddamn phone. Yes, there was a car accident. Please hurry, the girl's hurt badly. We're at..."

Prudence couldn't stay conscious anymore. She let herself slip away. Her vision filled with white shuddering spots.

A gaggle of voices and lights brought her back to reality.

She opened her eyes and her vision slowly cleared. There was a faint high-pitched sound coming from the outside of what looked like a metal box filled with things she didn't recognize. A man's face was hovering over her.

She wanted to jump up and scream. The pain she was in as soon as she moved reminded her that this wasn't the dream she had.

"My name's Mike. Glad to see you're back with us. You had an accident and broke some bones. You're also dehydrated and malnourished. I gave you something for the pain. Nod if you can understand me."

Prudence was too scared to do anything but nod. The man was all smiles and soft gestures.

"We'll be coming into traffic as soon as we come to the main road." A woman's voice came up from behind her, startling Prudence.

"It's okay; it's okay." Mike reached over, trying to calm his patient down. Prudence's gaze shifted to Mike's jugular. Her glance focused on a vein on the side of his neck. Her vision tunneled, and all she could hear was the man's heartbeat. She could feel her mouth filling with saliva.

She tried to figure out why her stomach started growling. A strange smell filled her nostrils, making her even hungrier. Mike stared at her face, wide eyed. He pulled back, falling off his seat.

Prudence lifted her arm and touched her lips. She felt a twinge of pain. Something sharp had dug into her bottom lip.

She looked at her hand and realized the smell that was making her hungry was the blood from her lip.

It was red and… pretty. She couldn't think of anything else.

Mike opened his mouth to speak, but before he could, Prudence flew up from the gurney. She grabbed Mike's arm and yanked him towards her, feeling it crack under her grip. Mike hit her in the face with his other hand. Prudence took the punch, stumbling onto the gurney. She was focused on using her other arm to clench around the man's throat. Anything to prevent him from screaming.

She missed, but her hand was close enough to slash the man's throat with the claws extended from her fingers. Mike ripped his arms away from Prudence's grip to cover his wound, gurgling. He stumbled back, right into the ambulance's corner. The sight of blood spilling over his shirt made Prudence fly into a rage.

"Mine," she growled and tried to grab the man's face. He tried to push her away from him, aiming for her injuries. Prudence didn't care about the pain. All she wanted was right in front of her. She tackled Mike, her hands slashing all over his body, desperately trying to keep him still. She pinned his legs under herself and swatted Mike's arms away. Gripping the man's chin, her claws sticking in the flesh part under the jaw bone, she exposed the wound she caused on his neck.

"You okay back there?" The woman spoke again.

Prudence sank her teeth into Mike.

Warm blood rushed into her mouth and flooded her throat. Mike was still trying to push Prudence away from him, scratching everything he could reach from his position. She could feel his hot breath on her arm, the sweat rapidly flowing out of his pores as he tried to worm his body away from her. Fear colored the smells exuding from him. As she drank deeply her body came alive. Soft cracking filled her ears, and she glanced at her arm. The broken bone shifted and set itself, healing under the skin. Mike slowly started struggling less and less. Then finally he went limp.

The woman in the front noticed the noise and glanced backward.

"What the hell?" The ambulance stopped with a screech. The woman scrambled for something in front of her.

Prudence's head snapped up. The next second, she had grabbed the woman by the hair. She yanked the woman backward through the little opening separating the two spaces, breaking the plastic divider.

The metal around the opening bent and the woman's bones cracked under pressure. When she tried to put a hand over her new victim's mouth, the woman bit her hand and hit Prudence in the stomach. Prudence sat down on the woman's torso, her knees exerting pressure on the woman's ribs. Prudence wrapped one hand around the woman's chin, while another one slid around the back of the woman's head. One sharp motion and the woman's neck snapped.

Prudence bent over, sinking her fangs into the woman's

neck. She could feel herself draining the blood out of the corpse's body. The soft hush was soothing.

The pain faded, and all Prudence could feel was the warm feeling of a full stomach. If she focused just enough, she could feel her body fixing itself. Muscles were knitting back together, and blood was retreating into the now no longer burst veins and capillaries.

When the body under her was empty, Prudence smelled the air. There was still blood left in the other one. She got up and walked over, breaking the body into pieces to get to the slowly coagulating blood. She ripped the rib cage out and bent over, intoxicated by the smell.

A few minutes later, both bodies on the floor of the ambulance were completely drained. Prudence was sitting next to Mike, licking her fingers. Her light blue dress was soaked with blood, as were parts of the floor. She was trying to eat as much of it as possible.

After a few moments, Prudence heard a rumble outside. A lower sound than the wailing projected from the metal box she was in. Her hearing was enhanced by her feral state, she heard something slam and a heartbeat come within range.

CHAPTER THREE

Prudence walked over and pried open the ambulance's back door. A young woman, quite short, with extremely short red hair and freckles, was standing in front of a similar contraption as the ambulance, only differently shaped and red.

"Phew, I found ya. When I saw the mausoleum door, I ran as fast I could. Good thing Joe hadn't left after he hit ya." She looked at the inside of the ambulance and smirked. "Have a good snack?"

The woman's heart was steady, and she didn't even flinch when Prudence growled at her from the shadows. It made Prudence want to stand back and observe instead of attack.

"I'm going to give ya something that belongs to ya. But try and make me a meal and you'll wake up with a massive headache." The woman removed what could have been a gun if Prudence squinted hard enough, from her shoulder. She put her hand in her pocket and tossed something out. It glinted in the sun and landed in front on Prudence.

Prudence knelt and snatched it out of the patch of sun. It was a necklace — a soft chain on which there was a pendant. The top of the tear-shaped pendant was rough and felt unfinished. She had a vague recollection of this being around her neck and the feeling of it on her skin. When she turned it around, she knew the initials P. D. would be there. They were a bit faded but still legible.

The fog lifted, and Prudence felt the familiar feeling of knitting needles boring into her head again.

She was crawling over the bloody floorboards again. But this time she could see around her. The house was small, and in shambles, the walls around her splattered in red. The man above her was graying and menacing, heavy-set, but unencumbered by it. Prudence saw herself rip off the necklace from her neck. And then her vision turned red.

The pain subsided, and Prudence fell from the ambulance to the ground. Breathing heavily, she rose.

“Who am I? Who are you?”

“The first question is too complicated to be answered here. Second question – I'm Charlotte, and ya were in my great great Aunt Prudence's grave. I got a letter telling me to keep an eye and take care of ya when ya wake up."

“Why?” Prudence tread lightly.

"How the hell should I know?" Charlotte shrugged. "The important thing, for now, is for me to help you hide those dead bodies."

Prudence turned around. She opened her mouth in horror as the faces of her victims stared back at her. She could recall everything she did in visceral detail. Every sound, smell, and taste. Half of her wanted to throw up. The other was sated and content.

Prudence realized she could still smell the blood on her hands. She started wiping them on her dress. Tears rolled down her face. Her mind focused on the victims' terrified expressions. She took their lives, she tore through their bodies and relished it.

Before she could realize it, she had sat down on the ground, hugging her knees. The screams tumbling down from her throat were ones of an animal in pain.

Charlotte approached her. "What's gotten into ya?"

Prudence looked up. Charlotte's expression was horrifyingly calm. "What has gotten into me?" Prudence pointed at the ambulance. "I did that! I took another person's life!"

Charlotte blinked several times. "The letter said ya've been hit with a bout of amnesia, but you seriously don't know why you did that?"

Prudence got up, walking over to Charlotte. She towered over the small redhead. "Why did I do it? Tell me!"

Charlotte took a deep breath. "I guess we're doing this

here after all. One of ya parents is or was a vampire. Ya know what a vampire is, right?"

Prudence stepped back.

“Ya not only spent several centuries stuck in a stone box, occasionally moved, with no food or water, ya got hit by a car going 50 miles per hour. The guy that hit ya, Joe, said ya flew out of some bushes, and most of your body was mangled. It’s obvious ya were probably on the brink of death. Instincts happen.”

“That’s all you have to say?” Prudence yelled. She looked at the road, at the trees around her. The vision of the hanged woman floated back into her mind. “I shouldn’t be alive.”

Now it was Charlotte’s turn to yell. Her high-pitched girly voice carried a surprising amount of weight. “No, ya don’t. Ya’re going to get into that truck before the sun makes ya get blisters and I’ll clean this up. How could ya have stopped if ya didn’t even know what you were? And don’t even try and sneak out, I have good aim.”

"You really think that will hurt me?" Prudence eyed the gun.

"Ya're still half human, and these darts can put down an elephant." Charlotte pointed at the truck behind her. "Go, now."

CHAPTER FOUR

Prudence didn't believe Charlotte, but the idea of hurting anyone else made her sick. When she thought of running, she realized she had no idea what would kill her. Or how long before she flew into a haze like that again.

Prudence skulked over to what Charlotte called a truck. Charlotte opened the door for her. She then reached under Prudence's seat and pulled out a metal container.

"Here, it seems ya have a little way to go with healing still. Don't worry; this is a pig. I got it from the butcher's shop."

Charlotte unscrewed the lid, and the smell reached Prudence's nostrils. She recoiled. It definitely smelled different from the blood she had before.

Her stomach growled.

“I don’t want it.” Prudence could still taste her two victims in her mouth. She wanted nothing more than her taste buds to stop working.

"Look, this is better than accidentally killing more people right? We know how ya get when you’re hungry."

Prudence picked up the container and drank from it. It tasted delicious, which is exactly what she didn’t want. It didn’t compare to human blood, and that was what made her even more scared. What if I attack others? How can I stop myself? Thoughts like that were swirling in her head. She looked down at the thermos. At least with this, I didn't hurt anyone. The pig was already dead. And the taste wasn't that different if she squinted really hard.

When Prudence was finished, she finally spoke. “What else do you know?” She felt her voice break.

“After we get away from the murder scene.” Charlotte wagged her finger. “Let me finish cleaning up first.”

* * *

CHARLOTTE DIDN’T STOP TALKING for all the time it took her to methodically clean everything and set the scene up to look like an accident. “We had fancy things in 2015. Ya drained them, but there is still hair, stuff under their nails, and even fingerprints. Ya touch something, we know ya touched it.

But if we do this accident well enough, none of that will matter. Boy, ya did a number on this dude."

Most were incredibly detailed information about what she was doing and why. And some were comments which made Prudence uncomfortable. She didn't pay attention to most of it since it flew over her head. But she did learn they were in a small town in a place called Maine. The ambulance was set to catch on fire and dropped off the cliff, with the two bodies set inside. When that was done, both women sat in the truck and drove off.

"So, we can talk now." Charlotte was the first who broke the silence.

Prudence wanted to ask a hundred questions at once. "What do you know about me?"

"Well, I went off to study a few years ago, to get my degree — yes, women do that now, then I get back, and my family is dead. Only me and my cousin left. I get a letter in the will, saying that I need to keep an eye on a half vampire, half human put to sleep in the mausoleum by some dude. To hide ya. All I know is that my ancestors needed something very important. Otherwise, they wouldn't have made the deal. Also, it means people might try and kill ya." Charlotte drove at high speed, never looking away from the road.

"I was hidden?"

"Yeah, I don't understand it. Either a few centuries in a coffin somehow made ya stronger, or we're damn lucky vampires aren't out and about."

“So you know nothing about me? My name?”

“Nope.”

Prudence knitted her eyebrows. Charlotte was like a strange assault to her senses. She dressed crazily and talked loudly. Prudence understood maybe a little over half of what she said. She did things Prudence expected of no woman, seemingly without fear.

“I suppose the world has changed a lot since the 1600s.”

"Ya have no idea. Hazy summary: we colonized this continent and killed a bunch of natives and have been real jerks to them since, then we got pissed at England and fought in a revolutionary war and became the United States, then we went crazy again, split in two, fought each other, then merged back, stopped the whole slave thing, then the world went crazy twice more, and a bunch of people died, then slowly we started getting a bit saner and gave people other than white men the right to vote. Now we're advanced but still crazy. I think that sums it up." Charlotte lit a cigarette.

Prudence wrinkled her nose at the smoke. “Those are bad for you.”

"Duh," Charlotte smirked.

A few moments of silence later, after Charlotte had finished her cigarette, she spoke again, "By the way, for ease, ya can keep using Prudence as your name; until we find yours that is. I'll tell people ya're my cousin for now."

“Alright.” Prudence nodded.

Charlotte took a hard right and stopped at a large house. “This is it. Let’s go.”

Prudence didn't realize how much her surroundings changed until she got out of the truck. They were on a largely smooth and gray street, larger than Prudence had ever imagined a street could be. All the buildings around her were the same color. Spacious, white-walled stores or houses. Prudence felt small.

"Over here lady!" Charlotte snapped her out of her thoughts. She covered Prudence with a blanket she removed from the truck, along with all her other things. Prudence remembered the crusty blood on her clothes.

CHAPTER FIVE

Prudence was shocked at how she could recognize the house's style. It has obviously been heavily rebuilt, but it was clear they kept as much of the original as they could. The outside was painted white, with a dark roof, a tall metal fence around a medium sized yard with a bench under an apple tree in it.

When they came inside, Prudence saw a long hallway with stairs leading up to the second floor, her now bare feet comfortable on the plush red carpet. Charlotte led her through a side entryway. That area was divided into two parts, both with cream walls. One had a balcony and very large windows taking up the largest wall. Every piece of strange furniture was light. Apart from a large black rectangle above the fireplace.

"Living room, where we sit around." She then swiveled Prudence around and led her to the other side of the room. "Kitchen, where we eat. Aka, stuff ya're not using until ya know how. Food's in those cupboards, and here. Fridge keeps it cold. There's blood in there too." She opened a large green cupboard Prudence noted was called a fridge. She didn't try and touch anything. She could learn about them when Charlotte wasn't running around and could help.

“I have to go to work now, but you won’t be alone.” Charlotte walked back to the stairs and screamed. “Milo, get your ass down here now! Letter business!”

After several loud thumps and a few hushed "I'm coming," a tall, scrawny man came down the stairs. He had messy brown hair, a square jaw and small blue eyes hidden behind large eyeglasses with very thin frames. When he saw Prudence, he quickly wiped his hands off his long gray sweater, smoothed out his hair and offered a handshake. "Oh, you're awake. Milo Davenport, nice to meet you."

“Yeah, yeah, yeah. Ya’re on babysitting duty. Lose her, ya die.” Charlotte interrupted them.

“Yes, ma’am.” Milo did a salute.

“Don’t be a snarky jerk.” Charlotte punched Milo in the arm and left. As the door closed, Milo turned to Prudence, extending the handshake again.

Prudence was frozen. Milo's face didn't look right. She found herself mentally adding some gray in his hair. Then a resigned exasperation with the world to his expression. Finally, she turned his eyes brown. She noticed his expression changed from politeness to confusion and to nervousness.

She shook her head. “That was odd.” She tried to explain herself.

“Um, what was?” Milo dropped his hand and put it in his sweater pocket.

“I think… you look like someone I knew. But I can’t remember who.” Prudence turned around, found a chair and sat down.

“Oh, well I hope it was no one that you dislike. Maybe it’ll come back to you later.” Milo smiled.

“I hope so too. With my luck, it’ll be just like all the other memories I’ve gotten today. Painful and violent.”

Milo rocked on his feet, and he was looking at the floor. Prudence could tell he was nervous, so she made an attempt to smile. He noticed and returned the favor.

“Do you need anything? Like, a change of clothes?” Milo offered, gesturing toward Prudence.

Prudence looked down. The blood on her blue dress made her sick. She nodded, trying to keep calm.

Milo scratched his head. “How about I show you where you’ll be staying? The darkest room, only one on the bottom floor.”

“That would be nice.” Prudence smiled. Milo seemed to be comfortable with her, but not comfortable with the fact he had been taken away from whatever he was doing on the second floor.

Prudence noticed his hands were calloused, but they didn't seem like calluses created from working with metal or wood. They were mainly on the middle finger, forefinger, and thumb. Prudence imagined what would make them be like that. She concluded Milo must spend most of his time writing.

"I guess being gone for a few centuries is a recipe for confusion huh? Don't worry you'll figure it out, and we'll help." Milo showed her the way and opened the door for her. Prudence was surprised that the gesture was familiar.

“Thanks." Prudence was in a room with dark blue walls and a fluffy green carpet. There was a bed with light blue sheets and a dark frame with a headboard, a desk, some chairs and bedside tables the same color as the bed frame.

Milo walked in and opened the only white door in the room. “This is the bathroom. Where we clean ourselves and, em…” Milo suddenly looked uncomfortable. He put one of his hands in his pant pockets and looked away. “It also serves as an outhouse.”

Prudence raised her eyebrows and went in after him. She was curious.

“Toilet, where you, um…” Milo trailed off again.

“Oh, I know that word.” Prudence was quick to ease Milo’s discomfort.

Milo smiled. “Okay, press here and water flushes out the

remains." He flushed the toilet. "It refills back again on its own. This is the trash bin, for trash, we empty it ourselves."

He turned and pulled back a strange curtain. "This is a bathtub, for cleaning. This is for hot water, this is for cold ; you turn them, and it comes out of here. If you need help, you can call me."

He turned again, this time to a small porcelain bowl sticking out of the wall, over which was a mirrored cabinet. "This is a sink, like a tiny version of the tub, used for face and hands. We shower every day now and brush our teeth with… something I need to get for you, hold on." He walked out.

Prudence looked at herself in the mirror. Her skin was tan and smooth. Her long face showed a sign of freshness she cringed at. She felt tired. Her eyes were large and brown, slightly upturned at the ends. Her hair was brown and long, up to her knees, and a bit dry at the ends. Her body felt limber, and her muscles didn't hurt. She also felt sated.

She wanted to feel terrible. She felt she deserved to. No one should have been able to gain this much through the death of others, and yet here she was, healthy as she could be, with two murders in her past. Closing her eyes, she could see them in her mind. Their eyes were full of fear.

When Milo came back, Prudence wiped away her tears.

"What's wrong?" He asked, looking around as if expecting to see a tangible reason in the bathroom.

Prudence sniffed. “Nothing, just, overwhelmed, I guess.” She didn’t want to dump her problems on him.

Milo looked at her like he didn't believe her. But instead of saying anything he gave Prudence a few small items. A small orange brush, a tube, what looked like a flat rough stick, and a pair of shears.

“This is a toothbrush, for brushing your teeth, and this is toothpaste, you put it on the toothbrush. This is a nail file, I noticed your nails might be hindering you, and scissors for your hair.”

Prudence looked down at her hands. Sure enough, her nails were long and cracked, snagging on her dress.

“We can get you to a hairdresser, a person that cuts hair for a job, later. Now I assume you would want a manageable length.”

"Yes, what length is customary now? Charlotte's is very short…" Prudence kept busy by turning the items Milo gave her over and over in her hands. The tube was smooth and squishy; the nail file was rough and flimsy.

“Umm, any actually. Women and men all have all sorts of hair lengths and styles. I don’t think you can go too short or too long when you cut it. Some even shave it.” Milo pointed to about his waist and then pointed to his own hair. “For clothes, we have a lot that might fit you. Your height and weight are pretty average.” Milo scratched his head. He was looking Prudence over, she noticed, but his glance wasn't disrespectful. "Not that you don't have the right to buy some later…"

He then produced another metal item from his pocket. "This is a nail clipper. Just put the nail in here and press down."

Prudence clipped one of her nails carefully to show she understood. After fixing those, she asked Milo to help her cut her hair. He did a decent enough job, cutting the driest parts of the thick strands, making her hair come to the middle of her back. Prudence instantly felt lighter.

"Now," she turned to the bath. "I turn this and — oh!" She turned the tap on, and the water streamed from the spoon-like thing resting on the tap, soaking her hand with slightly too hot water. Milo hurried and helped, flipping a switch. The water started flowing from the tap.

"Just turn it in small increments. I assume you'll be able to figure out the bottles?" He asked nervously.

"Yes." Prudence suddenly wanted nothing more than to remove the bloody dress. "Thank you. For everything, I feel more comfortable now."

"Not a problem, I am glad you feel better now. I'm going to go and let you, um, do what you do, but feel free to call me, for help." Milo seemed to notice that Prudence wanted to clean herself. He pointed her to the towels and told her where to find clothes before quickly leaving the room. Prudence was surprised at how kind, gentle and patient he was with her. She was glad.

After fiddling with the bath a bit, she sat down letting the warm water clean her body. There were bottles all around her, and fortunately, all had instructions and names on them. Things have gotten a lot more complicated than soap she thought.

When there was no more blood coming off of her, she filled the bath with water and sat back. Her eyes closed, and she let the heaviness she felt in her body consume her.

The knitting needles bored into her brain again. She felt a hand around her head, pushing her down. She couldn't breathe. She opened her mouth and gulped water into her lungs. She tried to move, but her hands were tied behind her back. All she saw was a whirl of foam and bubbles.

Prudence jumped out of the tub, hitting her hand on the wall. It took a few minutes to register exactly where she was. A few more minutes for her heart to stop beating so fast.

These memories were tiring her out. If she had to guess she'd say she had been asleep at least three hundred years. Who did that and why? Milo said that Charlotte would show her the letter when she came back. Prudence had two reasons for wanting the day to be over.

The idea that someone wanted her dead, and that the person might still be around if they were a vampire didn't fill her with as much fright as one thought it would. It was as if she had been used to it; it was familiar. When she took into consideration, all of the memories she'd gained were violent, that seemed logical.

Prudence got up, feeling trapped in the bath. She dried her body then opened the wardrobe, grabbing a bright orange long skirt and a button-down shirt she thought would work for now. The fabric they were made of was the least odd from everything in the closet. Prudence wound up her hair in a low bun and yawned. Her body ached for sleep, but she was scared that if she closed her eyes, another vision of her memories would show up.

Despite her brain's protests, her body found its way to the bed. It was unbelievably soft and smelled like flowers.

"Maybe the nightmares will stop if I'm comfortable." She murmured as she wrapped herself in the blankets and closed her eyes. She didn't know why, but she felt safer curled up in a fetal position.

CHAPTER SIX

An ornate cabinet loomed over her, the bottom of it was all drawers while the top was shelves behind doors. It was dark brown, with curved legs and vines carved into its doors. The doors were ajar, and it worried her. She ran to it. She could only reach the drawers, so she looked for a chair. Her weak little arms could only drag it over. She pushed it up to the cabinet and climbed up. Just as she was about to boost herself up and see what was missing, she woke up. She only saw her reflection for a quick second.

Prudence rose up, hearing Charlotte's voice. In the dark room, her eyesight was sharper. Was that a childhood memory? She thought as she got up and went to splash water on her face. She rewound the only pleasant memory she got so far over and over in her head.

When she looked in the mirror, she had thought that it would be good to know how her fangs worked. She didn't want to see them, but them showing up in public was worse than her being a bit uncomfortable.

Focusing on them, she opened her mouth and urged them to grow from her gums. The fangs were long, and thin, slightly curved toward her bottom lip, reminding her of a snake. She touched them, and winced, realizing how sharp they were. They were also still slightly stained. She assumed it was because she drank blood with them, and they retracted away from any saliva, food or drink that could remove the spots.

When she focused, she could see a small amount of what she assumed was venom dripping down them and into the sink.

Prudence took the toothpaste and brush and brushed her teeth. The sensation was odd, especially since the paste was aggressively minty. She stopped several times, certain it was burning her. But it was all worth it in the end. The paste took away all traces of blood in her mouth.

Prudence retracted the fangs and touched her teeth with her hand. They seemed normal otherwise, though she could feel the place where the fangs retracted into her gums, right in front of her canines. Unless one knew where to look, one wouldn't know there was anything different.

“Are ya awake yet? If not, get the hell up already. Didn’t ya get enough sleep?” Charlotte banged on the door.

Prudence winced at the loudness.

"Coming." The prospect of finding out more about herself and the man that put her to sleep made her rush out the door. Charlotte shoved a yellowed piece of paper in Prudence's hands as soon as she exited. She unfolded it and tried to read it out loud. Her reading was slow, and she had to stop at points, but it was more from lack of practice and the strangeness of some words than anything.

Hon, if you're reading this, it means I'm dead.

Now I know that's a cliché, but it's one for a reason. Now let me tell you the dirty family secret. Well, another one anyway. Don't worry this one's fun. Well, more fun.

A long time ago, our family was in a lot of trouble. I'll spare you the details; you would roll your eyes. But a nice young man, described to me as pale, tall and slim, with dark hair and eyes and a low, crumbly voice, offered a deal. He'd get us out of trouble, and all we needed to do is keep an eye on the woman currently with him. He planned to put her to sleep using magic and then have us hide her in a grave, moving her around with the times until she either woke up on her own or when he came to wake her.

Now, the woman was Asian, average looking, and couldn't remember anything about herself. She still gave him a run for his money when she overheard his plan. She tried to run away. He caught up to her so fast we didn't actually see him run. Though she was no pushover either. She put him through a wall. Despite that mess, he managed to put her to sleep and fixed the damage with a few words and a wave of his hand.

When he put her to sleep, he explained she had been hunted for who she was, a spawn between a vampire and a human. He didn't know why someone would destroy her memory, but he assumed she just needed time to recover, and sleep would help. He also explained he was, in fact, a vampire, which was apparently a huge secret. He might have been hunted and even killed just for telling us that. He gave us the locket you'll get with this letter and told us to keep it safe but avoid putting it on her neck.

He had told our family that if anyone like him appeared again, we were to use any holy symbol we could find to stave them off, toss them in the sunlight, or stab them with wood. Then set the corpse on fire. That we were to be careful because some could do a lot more than even he could, just by speaking. And that if we ever felt danger, we should take precautions.

Now I have never had the pleasure of meeting someone like that, and I honestly hope you don't either. But better safe than sorry. So when my gut shifted, and I saw strange people following us, I knew I had to do something to ensure you find out about this.

After the man had fulfilled his end of the bargain, our ancestors hid her. You had always wondered why every day, one of us goes to the mausoleum in the old graveyard. Or why most of our inheritance went to fixing the graves of our ancestors. This is why. We thought it would be safer than burying her. We're not aware if she could suffocate.

I don't know if the man is still alive, or if the deal still counts. But this has been a part of our history for almost three hundred years, so indulge us. And if she does wake up, make sure you keep an eye on her until he comes here to take her with him. If she survived that long, chances are he, and the people who wiped her memory did too. And that means you're in danger just because of association. You might as well have someone on your side.

I never did believe the guy was a vampire, let alone the girl's heritage, but I've seen her breathe in and out and felt her pulse, and that is enough for me to keep doing this. Move her within the next week or so after you read this, call Milo and everyone still alive, and keep together. And continue being your vigilant self.

Good luck hon.

Uncle Tim.

CHAPTER SEVEN

Prudence reread the part where the letter mentioned her a few times. For some reason, she didn't think it was her at first. Did she really attack someone so savagely? Why would she do that? The two dead bodies floated in her mind again. Of course, she would do that. This part of her, the one making her drink blood for her own survival, was the one making her do all those things. If she could somehow claw it out of her, she would.

Prudence realized she was standing silently for too long, so she frowned. "That's not that helpful."

"Well, at least ya know that ya're not a dainty little flower. That's always helpful when people are trying to kill ya." Charlotte handed Prudence a bowl filled with solid balls of brown, white and pink food. The bowl was cold. “Ice cream. Desert. It’s yummy.”

Prudence took the bowl and sat down in what they called the living room. The seats were comfortable and soft. All of them seemed to be pointed at the black thing hanging above the fireplace.

Milo reached for something on the glass table, but he stopped. He turned to Prudence. “Oh, I forgot to explain to you. This is a television. We figured out how to make moving photos. When I press this button, they will show up. But you need to understand that those are just moving photos, nothing more.”

“…Alright.” Prudence was confused. Milo was so serious.

“There are no tiny people inside,” Milo said.

Prudence raised her eyebrow. “…Alright.”

“Ya’re weirding her out dude.” Charlotte chuckled, hitting Milo on the side. “Ya know the fact people always think that in your stories, it doesn’t mean she will too.”

“Maybe not, but I like to cover my bases. There is no reason to scare her.” Milo turned on the television.

A loud sound escaped it, and Prudence was faced with what she expected. Moving pictures. The explanation didn't make it any less strange. But Prudence could understand how someone would think people were stuck in it. When she looked at the device, strange images from a book floated in her mind.

"Zahn." She spoke as if reading from a book.

"Huh? Are ya remembering something?" Charlotte moved from her seat as if to catch Prudence if she fell over.

"No. It's one of those things I already know." Prudence scrunched up her face. "Johann Zahn."

"Milo, ya know who that dude is?"

"Yeah, he invented the camera before technology caught up," Milo said, impressed. "How do you know about him?"

"I don't know; maybe I've seen or heard of him?"

"Or you've read the book." Milo got up and then sat down. "I would have said I can get it for you, but come to think of it, I'm not so sure. I'll check."

Prudence smiled. The rest of the evening devolved into Milo talking about cameras and Prudence listening. The ice cream had melted. Charlotte had left, but not before saying she'd be taking Prudence to town with her tomorrow.

Prudence hadn't even gotten used to the fact one could take her picture with just a tiny brick people kept in her pocket when Milo's eyes started to close.

"You can go to bed you know." She smiled at him. It was kind of sweet he was trying to keep her company.

"No, I want to keep you company, you don't have to be alone all night. I don't know why I'm already sleepy." Milo looked at the floor. "Oh, wait, I have something for you." He walked away and came back soon with a pile of white pages. "Vampire myths. Now I don't know how much of this is accurate, but this is what society has thought of them.

Considering we got the weaknesses right, there might be something else here that's of use. I included fictional accounts too. Most of the stories describe vampires as hypnotic, hungry beasts that can entrance their victims with their beauty but looking at you I don't really buy that. Not that you're not beautiful, it's just you don't seem like someone that would do that. You're nice." He stammered out.

"I understood that. Did you get that, from the..." Prudence couldn't remember the word Milo used to describe the latest piece of technology someone had invented.

"Computer and the Internet." Milo smiled. "You don't need to learn everything at once."

Prudence picked up the papers from Milo. "Thank you. I'll see you tomorrow. Get some sleep, you need it." She wanted to greet him, but she did not want to hug him, and a handshake seemed too formal. Instead she squeezed his hand as a greeting.

"Sure thing. If you need anything else, don't hesitate to ask me." Milo left to go to bed.

CHAPTER EIGHT

Prudence carried all the papers to her room. She sat down on the bed and set to reading them. She tried to read with the light on, but she had to turn it off. It hurt her eyes too much. That made her feel even more aware of her vampire side. And even more uncomfortable.

The night was spent wide awake, faced with things that made her flinch with disgust. The images she had seen were reminding her so much of the scene in the ambulance she had to stop several times to calm herself down. They were all gore and blood. Abominations crawling around on the ground after people, and well-dressed gentlemen hypnotizing young women.

All the references to unquenchable hunger made her go to the kitchen. She opened what she now knew was called a fridge. The door was too hard to open for her liking, and the cool air inside made her flinch. There were a few metal canisters labeled blood. Prudence picked up one and then turned around, wondering how to heat it up.

Not knowing how she called Milo.

He got up, his hair askew, and smiled when she apologized profusely about waking him.

He gently ushered her to the kitchen. There Prudence picked out a mug for herself. She poured some blood into it. She might as well get used to this. If she was going to control her hunger and not kill anyone else she needed to know.

Milo opened a small box-like thing, put a lid on the mug, and then put it inside. He then pressed a few buttons. Despite the fact he seemed sleepy he wasn't impatient, in fact, he was far calmer than Prudence was. For some reason it made her feel better about the fact she needed to drink that.

"When this beeps, open it and press this button to turn it off. Then take it out. Be careful it'll be hot. Okay?"

“You’re leaving me alone?” Prudence’s voice cracked. She didn’t want to mess this up and ruin the kitchen.

Milo smiled. "I'll be here; I just want you to do it yourself."

Prudence nodded. When Milo sat on a chair, she stared at the spinning mug and the numbers going down slowly. She could feel Milo was observing her, and if she focused hard enough, she could feel his heartbeat. It didn’t make her hungry if she thought of his face. The more they talked, the more his face was solidified in her mind.

After the microwave had beeped, Prudence jumped. She ran Milo's instructions over and over in her head as she attempted to retrieve her cup. The blood was nice and warm. Milo handed her a thin straw made from a strange material.

"Thanks."

"You're welcome. I'll go to bed now. Don't hesitate to call me if you need anything else." Milo made a move like he wanted to hug her, but when Prudence flinched, he just smiled and squeezed her hand.

Prudence nodded and went back to her room. She drank her blood as she read the list of things vampires might be vulnerable to.

Reading people talking about half of her as a myth was a strange out of body experience. She tested a few things out and realized her instincts still remembered dangers. Crosses made her uncomfortable and dizzy, as she figured out when she walked around and found one in a room. The sun felt as if someone was pouring uncomfortably hot water on her. She didn't have a way to test the wood bit. And honestly, she didn't want to. Silver didn't have an effect on her skin.

When she read the theory that the vampire myths could be mistaken for a disease called Porphyria, the first thought she had was how much she wanted to have it. But when she read on, she realized she couldn't have it.

Prudence closed her eyes and started repeating to herself.

"I'm not a monster; I'm not a monster. I can stop myself; I won't be a threat. I'm not a monster…"

Later, she fell asleep on the bed, surrounded by papers. Her dreams were flooded with photos from the papers around her.

CHAPTER NINE

Prudence agreed to go with Charlotte to her job the next day.

"I have an idea on how to keep ya safe. I'll get ya a job in the most secure building in town." Charlotte was throwing things from her bed in her handbag.

"And that is?"

"The police headquarters. They're the people who hunt law breakers; they're called cops. Which means they're armed."

Prudence's mind brightened at the description. She imagined noblemen, and probably women if Charlotte's speech in the truck was to be believed, protecting people from creatures like her.

“But, how will you explain me? And the fact I don’t know how things work?”

"The main boss, the sheriff, owes me a favor. Also, a sad story about my cousin who lost all her memory in an accident and is here to recover because no other family is left." Charlotte put her hands on her hips and smirked.

“You’re going to lie?”

“What do you want me to say? The truth?”

“Oh, right.” Prudence looked down in embarrassment.

“Come on.” Charlotte wrapped a hand around her. “Let’s get you dressed.”

CHAPTER TEN

The county morgue was right next to the police headquarters. They stopped right in front, and Charlotte led Prudence inside.

Prudence was walking stiffly. She hadn't worn pants before, and the fabric they were made of was rough and rigid. But keeping all her limbs covered and adding a hat made the sun bearable. Also, the dark blue jeans, like Charlotte called them, and the black blouse seemed to fit her well. The shoes were comfortable, though odd. Charlotte called them sneakers.

In the building, there was a flurry of people. Prudence was busy trying to recognize everything Charlotte described in the crash course about 'things you'll find at a police station.' Badges, guns, uniforms, files, computers. It wasn't going too well.

She realized that while the faces were moving too fast for her to remember all of them, their unique scents were easy.

Charlotte brought her to an office. There a short bald large man sat typing on a computer with two fingers.

"Hey, Rick." Charlotte motioned for Prudence to sit down and then plopped on the chair next to her.

"Good morning Miss Davenport. May I ask why you're here?"

"Well, I need a favor." Charlotte leaned in. "This is my cousin Prudence. She's my only other family besides Milo. She was coming over to visit us a few months ago and got in an accident. Lost her memory. Completely. Now, she used to live in Boston, but she has no one that can take care of her at all hours of the day there, so she moved in with me."

"Oh, I do hope you're alright." Rick extended a hand to Prudence. She shook it and flashed a polite smile. She kept herself from saying anything as to not ruin her chances.

"Now, I was hoping she can spend her days here so that she can do things that will stimulate her. Ya need someone to file the old documents anyway. Ya can pay her half the usual pay."

"And we'll be even?"

"Yup."

Rick turned to Prudence. “You’re hired. Charlotte, show her what she’ll be doing.”

Prudence was surprised it wasn’t harder. When they left, she broke her neutral expression by raising an eyebrow. “That was fast.”

“He doesn’t like owing me, and everyone hates that job. By the way, good job back there. I guess you’ve had a lot of practice pretending.”

The statement made Prudence sad.

Charlotte led Prudence to a small door leading to a large room with metal file cabinets, shelves with random things on it, and a small desk in the middle of it all.

"Basically, remove a file from the cabinets, make sure every single thing on the list I'll give ya is there. If it is, alphabetize it, that means take the last name of the officer in charge of the case and order them in an a,b,c order. If not, write what is missing and put it in a pile next to the desk. Later ya'll have the fun job of digging through more files and matching the missing things to the files. Don't worry if ya mess up."

Prudence listened carefully. It sounded easy enough. “That’s it?”

“If that seems easy, it'll give ya an excuse to look over cases, and ya'll have complete access to research anything and poke around." Charlotte leaned on the door frame. "Plus, people here will jump at the chance to help a cute amnesiac.

Come and see me when ya have your lunch break, so ya don't lug blood around."

Prudence needed time to get used to her surroundings. Pens were strange to hold and write with, and the room felt cold. She could feel the differences between papers over the years as she leafed through. She worked in total darkness but quickly turned on the desk light when someone would enter, to keep appearances. She found it was easier to understand things in context rather than just having someone explain them.

A young man brought her coffee. A few people entered to leave or take things they needed from the shelves.

Prudence read through gruesome murders, boring robberies, and domestic disputes with the same expression of horror. So many deaths, so much suffering.

The first time she got a headache, she bit her lip because she didn't want to scream and alert people. Flashes of a person with their head on backward filled her mind. She found herself curled under the table.

The next time it happened, she ducked under there right away. The tight space felt safe. She scratched up the floor under the desk as she struggled to push away the visions of a flogging, and nearly threw up when a man was pulled apart by horses. Lunch couldn't come soon enough.

CHAPTER ELEVEN

When lunch came around, Prudence left the room and made a beeline to the coroner's office. She came in just as Charlotte, dressed in what looked like a blue plastic bag, her hair under the same type of cap, and gloves on her hands, using a big version of what Milo said were pliers to snap the ribs of a corpse in front of her.

Charlotte chuckled at Prudence's expression of horror. "I do have to do this if I'm trying to find out how they died."

Prudence shook her head. "I understand that. It doesn't make it any less disturbing." The room smelled vaguely delicious. Prudence shoved that away from her mind.

"I have a degree saying I can open 'em up and poke around," Charlotte smirked.

"Oh, the files are over there. I'll finish up here, and we

can talk." Charlotte pointed at a pile of files with her bloodied hands.

It bothered Prudence that all other Davenports died within a week of each other. Charlotte, being the only Coroner in town, was the one to examine the bodies. Despite being forced to come to the conclusion the deaths were natural, she wasn't convinced. So when Prudence offered to look at everything, Charlotte quickly jumped at the chance.

Prudence sat down on a nearby chair and looked through them while Charlotte pulled out organs and measured them. She spoke in a small device Prudence assumed was noting her voice. The cause of death was apparently drowning in liquor.

Prudence found looking at these files easier. She could focus on the fact she was helping a friend and not organizing some sort of death journal.

All of the Davenports had a different cause of death. A fall from the stairs, a heart attack, as well as diseases she didn't recognize. "I don't know how I can help when I have no idea what all of this means."

"I'll explain everything. I also have samples and photos ya can see." Charlotte plucked something from the body and placed it on a tray. "I don't expect to solve this in a day. Or for ya to find something I didn't see just by looking at the files. I'm smarter than that."

"I will say, even to me this timing is strange. Each of these people has died within a week." Prudence felt her stomach growl. The hunger returned, and she wanted it gone as soon as possible. “You don’t have some blood by any chance?”

“Green thermos in the fridge." Charlotte pointed to her own thermos on a table, "looks like this," then at a similar box like the one in the house, only light blue.

CHAPTER TWELVE

Prudence picked up the thermos. She saw someone entering the office in the peripheral end of her vision, so she turned around, seeing a side door down a short hallway. It seemed to lead outside.

She opened it and sat outside in the shade, drinking her food. The outside was all brown, and it smelled rather bad. Prudence realized it was because there was a place to throw garbage out there, a large green metal box. It was tolerable though, especially when she didn't stand downwind.

"Fresh air, privacy, or smoke?" A male voice came from behind the corner.

Prudence wiped her mouth before the person came into view.

He was shorter than her, but buffer, dressed in a police

uniform, with long black hair coming down his shoulders. He was walking way too nonchalantly.

"Lunch. Soup." Prudence observed the man's movements. There was something about him that made her feel unsettled.

He walked slowly and deliberately towards her, standing in front of her and a little to the side, half of his body in the sun.

“Soup huh? Chicken?”

The tone of his voice was so conversational that Prudence almost missed the stake coming towards her heart. She blocked it by extending her arm.

He shifted his weight. He grabbed her hand and flipped her over him, throwing her into the sun on her back.

Prudence felt her bones crunch under the force of the fall. She scrambled up and turned around, her instincts telling her she needed to get on her feet as fast as possible and fight to stay on them. She faced the man.

He was frowning, his eyes searching the roof of the tall building next to them. “The hell?”

Prudence wasted no time and ran towards the man. She tackled him to the ground, her hands going around his neck in instinct. She stopped herself from trying to bite down, not wanting to hurt him.

Her hands felt uncomfortably hot. The man put his arms between hers and hit them, making Prudence release her grip. He then pushed her off and got up.

His neck was covered in inky religious symbols. Prudence looked down at her hands and saw they were red.

The man hit her in the head and pinned her to the ground. The stake in his hand plunged into Prudence's ribs. He missed the heart and hit one of her lungs.

Prudence bit her lip, feeling the pain from the stake radiate through her body. He was trying to pull the stake out of her. If he did, she was sure he was going to hit her heart when he tried again.

Flashes of red passed over her half-closed eyelids. In a desperate attempt to save her life, she took a big breath and, using all of her strength, lunged up. Her forehead collided with his nose. The man leaned back and fell down.

The blood on her forehead burned her. Prudence tried to not focus on the pain.

The man was not phased for long. She tried to block his punches, but he was accurate. A leg sweep later she was on the ground again. She reached out her arms, her claws extending.

He grabbed her wrists and tried to twist them in an unnatural direction. He had dropped the stake, so she used her legs to kick it aside.

As tears formed by strain filled her eyes, she noticed a figure looming over them both. A loud clang echoed in her ears. The man nearly fell over. He released Prudence’s wrist.

Prudence didn't have time to dissuade herself. She

collided her hands with the man's neck. Her fingers buried in his flesh.

As soon as she was on her feet, she released the man.

In front of her was Charlotte, a heavy-looking red metal cylinder with a hose on the top in her hands.

“What in all humanity happened?” Charlotte started, but Prudence felt the all too familiar pain in her head, and she doubled over.

CHAPTER THIRTEEN

A memory flooded into her mind. A person was sitting on a table, leafing through an ancient book. The words ‘vampire hunter' flickered into view.

Charlotte’s voice pierced the veil of pain. “Prudence, what can I do?”

Prudence grabbed onto Charlotte, trying to stay conscious as another memory fragment buried into her like a lance. When the pain was done, she released her grip.

She then heard a heartbeat. And a groan.

Charlotte turned around, picked up the heavy metal cylinder and dropped it on the vampire hunter’s head. Prudence winced at the crunch.

“They just told me they found a police officer knocked

out in the bathroom." Charlotte picked up her weapon. "I assume this is the guilty party."

Prudence stood up, but stumbled, falling into the pool of blood around her. Her skin started to burn.

"Shit!" Charlotte yanked Prudence to her feet and shoved her in front of herself. Prudence's eyes turned glassy as Charlotte took her down a winding hallway, and then cold water flowed over her face and body. Charlotte helped her remove her blood-soaked clothes. She scrunched up her face as she helped Prudence remove the blood, preventing Prudence from receiving more burns.

Prudence stood in the shower, letting it rinse every single trace of blood from her face when Charlotte left. The burns over her arms, knees, and feet were hurting, blisters forming on her skin.

Charlotte came back with a large steaming batch of blood. Prudence's fangs extended as soon as the smell hit her nostrils.

"Here. Don't worry, the people I got this from are still alive."

Prudence grabbed the bottle and drank deeply for a good fifteen minutes, the bottle heavy in her hands. She took great care not to spill any, feeling she would need every drop. When she was done, she saw the burn marks had begun to heal.

"Ok now tell me what happened." Charlotte insisted.

"Vampire Hunter." Prudence felt the pain slowly die out.

Charlotte wrapped her in a blanket.

"And how did ya know that?"

“I remembered.” Prudence thought back. All she could see in her mind was a still of the book sitting on a table, and the page. “But it’s just information.”

"Okay, well, they are looking for the person that stole the uniform, so I better clean up the mess and then call them. Ya can tell me everything later."

“Charlotte, why is someone trying to kill me?” Prudence hugged her knees up to her chest.

“No clue, but I know I'm not gonna let them. Ya stay here, while I lie my ass off now. There are clothes on that chair."

Prudence observed the expression on Charlotte’s face. An overwhelming amount of guilt crashed into the forefront of her mind. Here she was, feeling sorry for what she was, while two people she had just met were ready to kill to keep her safe.

“Thank you for saving my life.”

“Eh, not a problem. Glad I picked up the fire extinguisher.” Charlotte winked. “Now, sit in there, while the officers leave.”

Prudence nodded. The more she stayed away from people, the better.

CHAPTER FOURTEEN

She got into the loose-fitting clothes Charlotte got for her. She then sat back on the chair. She was here for two days, and a vampire hunter stole a lawmaker uniform and tried to kill her. And now he was dead. Which meant his friends would know, and what was stopping them from coming after her too?

Prudence felt short of breath again. What did she do to have become hunted? She didn't know if it was because of her past or just because of what she was. But she was trying to control it! Or maybe they didn't know that? But then how did the hunter know where she was? A sudden realization that she had probably been followed here dawned on her. Then they knew about Charlotte and Milo.

Prudence stopped shaking and turned into a statue when Charlotte yelled for help. A large crowd of people ran in.

“What happened?” Rick’s familiar voice, with a string of worry, sounded out.

“The jackass that jumped Tom is back there.”

"What? Is he dead?"

“Someone made mash potatoes out of his head.” Charlotte’s voice was as calm as ever.

The crowd moved towards the back door. A string of curses and prayers rang out.

CHAPTER FIFTEEN

Prudence waited until she was sure no one was in the room she needed to pass through. She sneaked out and made her way to her room. Most of the cops were in Charlotte's office, so it was easy to run through. She needed darkness and quiet. Her body was still healing.

She closed the door and started breathing in slowly, trying to calm her heart down. She needed to calm down until she could talk to Charlotte, so she took a piece of paper and a pen then transcribed everything she saw on the page in her mind. After that she had to stop and read it back, finally knowing exactly what she faced.

Vampire hunters are a lot more complicated and dangerous than they appear. Never underestimate them. First of all, they are not supernatural creatures, but ordinary humans, armed with the skills they have accumulated during their time on this earth and an unending desire to destroy all of us. Again, do not underestimate them, or discount them, not even the new ones. They actively avoid being turned and don't care for their own life, fully capable of taking their target down with them.

To be truly able to pursue their prey, vampire hunters adorn themselves in religious symbols drawn by holy men, making their skin uncomfortable to the touch, or even causing burns. They also undergo a painful ritual that is said to purify their blood, making it poisonous and scalding to vampires. They possess extraordinary talents honed from years of training and are proficient in multiple forms of combat. They mostly use stakes, but they can modify them to be more efficient. Some even strike with arrows.

The mantle of a vampire hunter is usually passed down through a bloodline, but anyone who is determined enough can find a way to claim it. As such, the instance of the few survivors of a vampire attack can make several vampire hunters, even if most of them never truly reach that point, either dying during training or an early hunt. When something like this happens, an older vampire hunter who had been tracking the vampires inevitably appears and takes them with him.

This phenomenon, however, was more prominent in the times where vampires didn't hide their existence and walked freely. In 1002 AD it was recorded that only seven vampire hunters were still in existence. Records have become sparse since then as we have gone into hiding and can't observe them as closely. I predict that the more we hide and prevent the knowledge of us to spread the fewer threats we'll face.

"There ya are." Charlotte opened the door just as Prudence was done with reading. She carried a large file with her. "Ya healed well it seems. But then ya did drink about a gallon of blood."

CHAPTER SIXTEEN

Prudence turned on the light. When she saw Charlotte, all of her calmness evaporated, and she bolted up. She pulled her friend into a tight hug.

Charlotte chuckled, and when Prudence started crying, she patted her on the head. "There there. We'll get through this."

Prudence let Charlotte go and wiped her eyes. “You’re in danger just by being near me.”

“So? Ya didn’t ask for this, someone decided it for ya. The best we can do is find out who this dude was and make sure this doesn’t happen again. Do ya agree?” Charlotte waited until Prudence nodded.

“Okay, now ya mentioned something about a memory?”

“Here.” Prudence gave Charlotte the piece of paper.

"Wow, nice handwriting." Charlotte began reading.

"Yeesh." She shivered. "It's hard to imagine these guys exist. But it would explain what we found. Plus, we live in the era of information. It's hard to hide."

"What did you find?"

Charlotte picked up the heavy file from the floor and put it on Prudence's desk. "So many different names, so many warrants, and a thick family history of bat-shit craziness. Typical."

Prudence raised her eyebrow at the strange phrasing and skimmed through the file. She ignored most of what she didn't understand. "Five counts of murder?"

"A count is how many times ya've been charged with a crime." Charlotte moved behind the desk and stared at the page. "And that is only for one of his identities. He used different names in different states and countries. It will take a while to get everything. He's being pursued internationally."

"There is more?" Prudence couldn't believe it.

"Hey he's in his mid-40s, and his first crime was at 13. He's had some time." Charlotte nodded. "But we haven't gotten everything yet. Will take a while. What I wanted to talk to ya about was this." Charlotte dug into the file and pulled out a yellowed paper. A photo of a woman with long hair took up a quarter of it. It was an old arrest warrant. Prudence looked at the photo of the vampire hunter that tried to kill her. She could see a similarity between them.

"My guess is this is his mother. She was gunned down too early to be anything else, and as your memory said this is passed down through generations. I just hope he didn't have any siblings. At least not any living ones." Charlotte pointed down to the third page Prudence leafed through. "Can this be related to my relatives?"

Prudence read the piece. It was a file on a murder people have been trying to link to this woman. She had been seen leaving the scene. The man in question had suffered a heart attack. There was no proof of foul play.

"It could be. Can you get your hands on more information?"

"Yeah. It might take a few days or weeks. But in the meantime, I'll cut into mister vampire hunter. Maybe we'll find out more."

CHAPTER SEVENTEEN

Prudence spent the rest of the day resting. When her day was over, she made her way back down to Charlotte's office. Charlotte was sitting on a chair, in her regular clothes. When Prudence came in, Charlotte quickly got up.

"I'll get the tissue." Charlotte put her gloves on and opened a thick door.

"What is that?" Prudence pointed at the door.

"It's like the fridge back there and in the house." Charlotte pulled out a few vials with what Prudence assumed to be blood out. "Only colder. It can keep blood and other pieces of flesh from falling apart. I can freeze things too. It's fun when the things ya're freezing didn't come from the person who changed your diaper." Charlotte handed a vial to Prudence. "What do ya think?"

Prudence opened the vial and smelled it. She instantly recoiled. The blood had the unmistakable aroma of warm rusty metal.

"Ugh. This was in a person?"

"My uncle. I can't pinpoint why it smells like that. Every test I try turns out normal." Charlotte shrugged.

"Do all samples smell the same?"

"I don't' know. My nose isn't as developed as yours." Charlotte handed all the other bottles to Prudence one by one, noting Prudence's reaction on a piece of paper. She, in turn, opened each once and smelled them, responding after each one.

"Fainter, but yes. This one smells a bit stronger. This one is fainter again… They all smell the same, though. It's like you have left a rusted blade in the hot sun and then smelled it." Prudence gave the bottles back and sat down. "Not a very appealing scent."

"Rusted huh?" Charlotte raised her eyebrows. "I have no idea what that could be."

"Maybe a spell residue?" Prudence shrugged.

"How do ya figure?" Charlotte put all the vials back in the fridge.

"Well, we know some sort of magic exists because of the letter your uncle left you. And if it exists, it is logical it would leave some proof behind, even if most people would not notice it. Nothing passes through space without changing it in some way."

“Wow, that’s smart.” Charlotte looked at the clock. “Crap, we need to go.”

“Where?” Prudence watched as Charlotte removed her gloves.

“We need to get you some identification. Which means I need to go and pull some old family connections.”

“You don’t seem happy about it.” Prudence handed Charlotte her coat.

"Let's say; my family history is colorful. Milo and I are, I think, the only people in the family without a criminal record. Crime runs in the family." Charlotte put on her jacket. "What a way to be a black sheep huh?"

Prudence ignored the confusing phrase. “So we are doing something illegal?”

“Yup. Let’s go.” Charlotte opened the door.

“Do we have to?”

"Unless you want to explain why ya have no identity despite being alive, yes."

Prudence sighed and followed Charlotte.

“We need to get across town fast.”

CHAPTER EIGHTEEN

The two women drove for about three hours until they got to the edge of town. She watched the houses melt away. They were replaced by large objects Charlotte called buildings. Then the buildings melted away too and were replaced by even tinier simpler houses. Just then Prudence realized exactly how big the town was.

When she exited the truck, Prudence saw a house which looked patched together from a few different houses.

"What is this?" Prudence got out of the car and followed Charlotte to the entrance. It was chilly, and the wind was picking up.

"A den of crime. Or at least the vacation den of crime." Charlotte banged on the door with her fist, then kicked it once. When the door opened, Charlotte grabbed Prudence's hand and ducked inside, dragging Prudence with her.

"Are ya ready?" Charlotte immediately started talking.

Prudence saw a tiny man in his 50s standing in front of them. He had thinning hair and oversized clothes. He seemed harmless, and that was what made him unnerving.

He was sniffing and wiping his nose with his hand. "Come in."

After walking through the dark hallway, the inside was quite brightly colored. Many lights compensated for the sun setting outside. The room they were in was large. It held a ton of equipment. Prudence was sure even Charlotte didn't understand most of what was in every obscured corner.

"She the one you need this for?" The man hurried to the equipment and started pressing a few buttons.

"Yup." Charlotte sat down on an old couch. "Name, Prudence Davenport. My cousin. Her great grandma, my great great aunt, should have the same name. Lived some time in Boston."

The man knitted his brows. "No driver's license? And how legitimate you need this?"

"Nope. Enough to be able to live a normal life and not get stopped by a regular cop." Charlotte stared down the man.

Prudence was almost certain the man was going to say no. Until Charlotte took a deep breath and said that he would be 'cool with her family after this' and she would burn a file.

The man brightened and nodded. “Let us do it then.” He motioned Prudence to a place where there was a chair in front of a stark white wall. He turned on a lamp.

“He is going to take your picture with a camera.” Charlotte took off her sweater and gave it to Prudence. “Here, this will look better.”

CHAPTER NINETEEN

Prudence changed and then sat down. The man picked up a square technological thing and pointed it at her while looking through it. "Don't blink and look straight ahead."

Prudence did as she was told. A bright light flashed at her, then blinked a few times. The man put the camera on the table and connected it to a computer. After a few minutes of the man tinkering, she appeared on the screen.

Prudence felt weird to see herself. Unmoving, unblinking, and strangely stiff. She moved just to make sure she was still alive. Wait, am I actually alive if I'm a half vampire she thought. Prudence reached and touched her pulse points, feeling her heartbeat. I think I can consider myself alive.

The man clicked a few other buttons. "Prudence, I'm

going to ask you questions, and you and Charlotte will answer. They will help make what you need."

Prudence turned to Charlotte, who nodded. She caught herself knowing Charlotte would prevent the man from finding out something he didn't need to. "Alright."

"What is the age you want to be?" The man deadpanned.

Prudence shrugged.

"Write twenty-six," Charlotte answered instead. "Young enough to be believable with your appearance, old enough to be an adult."

"Height?"

"Five foot five," Charlotte responded again. "Weight, one hundred and thirty pounds approximately."

"Eye color?"

"Brown." Prudence sounded. She had an incredible desire to be in control of her life. Someone answering questions about her like this, made her feel sick. Even if this was Charlotte.

The man continued to ask simple questions like that, and either Prudence or Charlotte responded. Within an hour, Prudence had a detailed background. She was supposed to be born here, in the hospital, partly because the man had a way to make sure the hospital had records of that. She would be going to middle and high school here and then moving to Boston for college to get a masters in History. Apparently, a college student would be the best cover for her according to Charlotte.

"Now, you need to make an accident report. Retrograde amnesia caused by brain damage from a car crash. Hospital stays in Boston. That is the reason why she has 'moved' here. I'll cover the hospital here." Charlotte came close to the man, resting her elbow on his shoulder.

The man turned and raised his eyebrows. Charlotte turned to him and did the same.

The man sighed. "Your mother would be proud of you, as well as yell at you for promising me what you did."

"Let me worry about her yelling at me in the afterlife. Do your job."

"It'll take some time. A couple of weeks."

"A couple of days ya mean."

"Alright, a couple of days."

"That's perfectly fine. Just make sure that she can live with the identity and not get arrested."

"You'll need a doctor here to confirm the diagnosis."

"Oh, I'll have that covered." Charlotte turned to Prudence. "Speaking of that, I need to call someone, so I'll leave ya alone. Call for me if he is being creepy."

"Sure." Prudence nodded.

CHAPTER TWENTY

Charlotte chuckled and then pulled out her phone. While Charlotte was too far and the conversation on the other side of the phone too low for Prudence to hear, Charlotte's voice was easy.

"Hey, honey. Haha, ya know me so well." Charlotte was licking her lips, and her tone was strange. Prudence was surprised to see Charlotte flirting. That tone and realization made something click inside of Prudence's head. She had heard that tone before she might have even used it. She wondered who she flirted with.

"Sure, if ya do me a favor and examine someone for me. Well, yeah but I need a doctor who works in a hospital."

Prudence was focusing on the conversation, but still

paying attention to the man. He wasn't moving much, and not doing anything that made her instincts flare up.

Charlotte's tone was intriguing. Prudence could tell it was familiar to her. She might have done a similar thing herself when she was whoever she was before.

Charlotte chuckled. "Well, we might be able to do something about that. Okay, I'll call ya when we need to come in. And then, we'll see."

Charlotte put the phone down and turned back towards Prudence. Charlotte had an expression of triumph and something Prudence felt she would be able to identify, if she had her memories.

"Do you need us for anything else?"

"Nope." The man waved them off. "And no need to keep calling me, this is at the top of my list."

Charlotte smirked. "See ya."

CHAPTER TWENTY-ONE

Prudence and Charlotte got into their car and drove home.

"So now I'll have an identity? Like the ones the vampire hunter had?"

"Not really. Those are less thorough than yours. And ya don't have an actual identity to base yours on."

Prudence looked out. "I guess I never exist according to your world."

"What do ya mean?"

"From what I've seen, people who don't have any information about them in files or whatever computers access, don't exist. So that means I don't exist. Culture has changed a lot."

Charlotte gave Prudence a good long look. "Ya are finding this really hard huh? The whole, 'I've been asleep for a few centuries and woke up in a different world' thing."

"I think you have just answered your own question," Prudence smirked, but that soon faded. "It is also made far more difficult by the fact I don't know who I am. I have nothing to look back to. I feel like I'm floating in an endless ocean without anything to hold on to."

"I can't say I'll be there all the time. I mean I'm human, and I have only known ya for a few days. But I'll tell ya one thing. Even if ya don't have your memories, ya still have a ton of character. And ya're brave as all hell."

"And how do you know that?"

Charlotte laughed so hard she snorted. "Have ya seen ya these days? Ya keep going even if everything, even your own body, is telling ya to stop at times. That counts as brave in my book."

Prudence didn't know if this would be rude, but she had to ask. "So that man on the phone, he is your…"

Charlotte chuckled. "He wants to be mine and for me to be his and I do too at times, but I am too set in my ways for an extremely serious relationship. I've been the love 'em and leave 'em type for so long I wonder if I can even do anything else at times."

"You do seem to like him. According to your voice back there. At least I think you do." Prudence looked in front of her.

"You're right, I do. He is nice and puts up with me. And he will make sure you will get the things you need."

CHAPTER TWENTY-TWO

When Prudence and Charlotte came home, Milo was in the kitchen, cooking.

"Oh, you're home?" He put a tray on the counter. Prudence stopped and observed him standing there in an apron and incredibly proud of the thing he was making.

"Yes." Prudence could smell a strange aroma on her skin. She could sense it all day. It was in the air, everywhere. She suddenly understood why people bathed every day. The air was heavy and smoky. "I'll go clean up. And later you can explain why the air is odd."

"Not a problem. Though you won't like it." Charlotte sat down. "Gimme that food."

Prudence dumped the clothes she was wearing on the

bed and went into the bathroom. Her skin was still prickly on the places where she was burned by the blood. It was also slightly redder in those places too. She took care not to scrub too hard as she rinsed off the grime from the day and the heaviness from her mind.

CHAPTER TWENTY-THREE

When she came back, Milo and Charlotte had already finished eating. They had left some of her. Prudence didn't touch it, instead she sat next to them.

"So, why does the air smell different? And why wouldn't I like the reason?"

Charlotte pointed towards Milo, who started talking while gesturing widely.

"The air is polluted. By all the stuff we have used to build the things we use. Coal, the smog coming from factories—"

"Those are the places where we make a lot of one thing." Charlotte interrupted.

"And from cars. We burned coal, we used oil and then we have a lot of animals, and they produce a lot of waste, mining, normal everyday household things, etc. They all pollute the air so much that the protective cover—ozone, that is preventing the sun from burning us all to a crisp is also thinning."

Prudence sat there, dumbfounded. "That doesn't sound good, especially to someone who already doesn't like the sun." She started wondering how other vampires felt. Ones that have seen this happen.

"We are trying to fix it, and there are a lot of people making noise and funding projects. Though there are also a lot of people, who deny this ever happened." Milo shrugged. "I don't understand them myself but eh."

Prudence imagined vampires posing as humans in order to fix the protective layer. It was funny to think about. A creature who hunts humans for food being lauded as a hero protecting the environment.

“Oh, and I was looking through things you wouldn’t know, and I brought you a map of all the countries in the world.” Milo went to his room and got back with a large map which he unfolded while walking. “There are a lot of people in the world now, around seven billion.”

“Billion?” Prudence took the map and sat down on the couch again. After studying it, she smirked. “Well, I can tell you some people were turning in their graves when this map was made.”

Milo looked like he wanted to say something but

changed his mind, shaking his head. “So, I don’t know how to explain it better but…”

“There are too many people, too little or badly distributed food, our leaders are crazy and/or greedy, and we destroyed our air by not being advanced enough to know it was happening before it became too bad.” Charlotte summed it up.

"That is not really that surprising." Prudence shrugged. When she turned, and she saw Milo's confused expression she chuckled. "What? Don't tell me that in this age, one of so much information, you have a romanticized view of the past?"

“So, people were not more sensible then?” Milo looked like someone punched him in the stomach.

"An entire group of people thought they were better than others and used them as property." Prudence folded the map and put it in her lap. This was the first time she had felt bitter. "You don't exactly win a prize for that." She turned her attention to what she knew the world was like. "For every human, they are the hero of their story. It's hard to convince them otherwise. And I don't think other creatures are any different."

Milo slumped down on a chair, defeated. "So, we haven't evolved or devolved. Are we the same as ever with only a few values changed? That's kinda depressing."

“Sorry.” Prudence looked down.

“Oh, no you did nothing wrong, I just need to accept it.”

Milo looked at the map. “There are a lot of people in the world, there has to be something good coming out of that.”

"Maybe it's just we hear about more stuff now." Charlotte shrugged. "Kinda like, now I know how many people die in this town when I am the coroner. When I started, it seemed like an alarming amount. But now I know that it's like that everywhere, and it's not really abnormal. Also, assholes make a lot of noise when they don't get their way."

"I think a lot of people feel that way when they are in a new situation." Prudence reopened the map. "With so many people in one place, it's normal." She still couldn't figure out how seven billion people fit in the world.

Milo shrugged. “I still want to believe we are doing better.”

"Well, you probably are. You haven't destroyed the world yet." Prudence looked at the semi-cold food on the table and took a bite. It was spicy and unusual, but it felt good to have something in her stomach other than blood. While she ate, the conversation lulled.

CHAPTER TWENTY-FOUR

Charlotte broke the silence by getting up and fetching desert. "I guess blood only goes so far huh?"

"Well, we know from the letter I'm half human. It makes sense that I can't survive on blood alone."

"How would that work anyway?" Milo pushed his glasses up his nose by the glass. "I mean, how were you born if a vampire is, how we've believed, a dead body with no heartbeat and hence no functions that would make a baby?"

"How it is possible that a body can walk and talk and knock someone out without being alive? Blood doesn't have that much power." Prudence said between bites of desert.

"Supernatural beings are supernatural Milo." Charlotte

shoved her cousin lightly. “It stands to reason they don’t act naturally.”

"There is probably an explanation, just like there is one about your relatives' deaths. It's just not something well known." Prudence shrugged.

"Well, I know that I'll have a long day tomorrow examining mister acid blood." Charlotte yawned and stretched. "And that means I want to sleep now, so I don't fall over tomorrow."

“Who is acid blood?” Milo squinted his eyes.

“The vampire hunter dude I told ya about. The one we killed.”

“Oh yeah, I made you stop describing because you were making me sick. That hasn’t changed.” Milo imitated a gagging noise.

“Don’t worry I won’t be here for this. She can catch ya up and spare you the details.” Charlotte ruffled Milo’s hair and left.

Milo took a deep breath. “Okay, tell me.”

"Vampire hunter attacked me; Charlotte killed him. His blood acts like acid on vampires." Prudence thought that was the best way, to sum up, everything. She didn’t want to make Milo uncomfortable. "Oh, and I also got a memory piece back. A page out of a book. I think Charlotte has it, hold on." Prudence got up and opened Charlotte's purse, digging through the mess until she found the paper, neatly folded up in a pocket.

Milo read the text carefully several times. “Well, this sounds like it was written by a very old vampire, just by the way the text references the past and how it seems to speak from experience and how it aligns itself with the vampire side. Also, that is a very detailed memory.”

“I think I was reading the book.” Prudence thought back. “Because I could see it very clearly. And the book was not new, and it was handwritten.”

“Incredibly detailed.” Milo moved to sit next to Prudence. “Did just seeing the vampire hunter jog this?”

“I saw the marks on his body. The tattoos. And I had my claws in him.”

“But, his blood was acid, no?”

“Yes, I got burned.”

“Then how are you fine now?”

“A lot of human blood can fix burns or the results of sitting for centuries in a coffin.” Prudence looked down. “Charlotte had some in her fridge.”

"That's... fortunate, despite you not liking it. I really hope you don't need blood that badly again." Milo put the paper down on the table. "Maybe the vampire hunter was working alone?"

"If he was, the question is how did he know I was one? His first method of killing me was dropping me in the sun. He didn't seem to know I was half human. Granted I am making an assumption, but his expression was too confused to count out. Which means I need to find how he knew and try and make sure no one else does. On the other hand, if he isn't working alone, it means I'm being hunted."

Milo sat back. "I am only listening to this, and even I'm anxious. I can't imagine how you feel. Though, figuring out how vampire hunters know you are a vampire sounds easier than being hunted."

"But if I'm not being hunted that would mean the vampire hunter is not connected to anyone who would know who I am. Which means the chances of finding out who I am, dwindle by the day."

“Ah.” Milo straightened up. “That makes it more complicated.” He yawned.

“You don’t have to stay up with me. You can go to bed. I might too.” Prudence lied. She knew her body needed some sleep, but she woke up yesterday after only four hours. She just wanted that time alone she would get to settle her thoughts.

Milo looked relieved. “Okay, if you want me to. But call if you need anything.”

"Sure."

CHAPTER TWENTY-FIVE

Prudence got up before everyone, despite the fact she went to bed late. When Charlotte got up and went to make coffee, Prudence had already started drinking her dose of blood for the morning. Pig blood tasted vastly different from human. Prudence thought to herself how the former was better, but the thought was uncomfortable. She focused on the delicious aspects of the blood in front of her instead.

When they got to work, Prudence, under the excuse of checking if her cousin was alright after yesterday, came with Charlotte to the morgue.

Charlotte changed and immediately went to open the vampire hunter's body. But when she opened what seemed like a metal drawer to Prudence, she didn't find anything.

“What the hell?” Charlotte bolted out of the door, screaming at the other people working in her building. Rick was there in just a few minutes.

“I was hoping that I’d see you before you found out.” Rick seemed agitated and sweaty. Prudence could see he had just come in because he was still in his coat. And she could tell he rushed getting here this morning because he seemed to have skipped shaving.

“What the hell happened to the body?”

“Feds came in and took it. Along with everything we had on the case.” Rick’s voice was low. He was faking being calm.

“And why would they want it?” Charlotte put her hands on her hips.

“The hell should I know? Two people in suits came in, showed credentials, which I checked, twice.” Rick stopped Charlotte from interjecting. “And then they packed everything up and left.”

Charlotte took a deep breath. “I trust you made sure they didn’t take anything not connected to that case?”

“Kept my eyes on them the whole time. They took your case file. Our case file. All the photos off the computer and the printed ones. The body and all swabs you took. The clothes, hell they even swept the back alley." Rick finally let his frustration show. He was rubbing the back of his neck and clenching his jaw in between sentences. "They said it was a part of an ongoing investigation. They even grilled me about what I know about you and your family."

Charlotte and Prudence locked eyes. Prudence felt a sinking feeling in her stomach. As much as she wanted to know who she was, she didn't like the idea of being hunted anymore than anyone else.

"What did you tell them?" Charlotte glared at Rick.

"Names, address, anything they'd find in a phone book. I muddled through your cousin here, since I don't know a lot as is. They asked for a detailed account of what you saw; I gave them the report. I refused to call you in the middle of the night for them." Rick then let out a grin of triumph. "I also didn't tell them your cousin is working here, or that you copied most of the files we had on the dude yesterday. Or about the house visit."

Charlotte raised her eyebrows. Prudence froze. Her mind ran around trying to find the best way to hide what Rick knew and get away. She only snapped out of it when Charlotte continued talking.

"I'm not up to my family's old tricks. I want ya to know that."

"Oh, I know. But it's beneficial to keep those links alive sometimes." Rick smiled. "And I can see that there is something more here. You might not want to tell me, and I'm fine with playing the dumbass here. The less they think I know, the less the chance I'll get hauled off along with the body next time."

“Remind me of this near Christmas.” Charlotte extended a handshake to Rick. “I should move ya up the shopping list.”

"Just don't die or get arrested. You keep people in line and have almost no life aside from your job. You're the best Coroner this town has ever had." Rick accepted the handshake and left, nodding to Prudence in greeting.

“What was that about? Also, what’s a fed?” Prudence asked as soon as she and Charlotte were alone.

“A nickname for a different type of cop. As for Rick, he’s known me since I was five. He was also the one who knocked some sense into mom when she was objecting to me going away for school. I’m glad he was the one here when those assholes showed up.” Charlotte came closer. “Ya think they came at night because they wanted to throw us off guard, or because they can’t actually walk in the sun?”

“Either way, we know chances are they didn’t just pick the body up because of the reason they gave. The more likely option is they were hiding it.” Prudence looked Charlotte up and down. “If they know about me, they most likely know he lied. If they don’t, they have enough to consider you interesting.”

“I better call Milo.” Charlotte took out her phone. When Milo answered with a cheery hello, she immediately started talking.

“We have a situation. Lock up and be on guard. I mean

it." Charlotte didn't wait for Milo to respond, she just terminated the call.

"That was brief."

"It's code. If I talk more than that and employ any niceties or don't say I mean it, he should assume I'm being held at gunpoint somewhere and haul ass."

"One of these days you are telling me what your family was doing." Prudence turned to the door.

"It would take too long." Charlotte returned to her work. "Suffice to say not a lot of them were nice people."

"But you are."

"Cause I like it more that way. And while my family's history does give me a lot of problems, it comes in handy for stuff like the things we did yesterday."

Prudence said bye to Charlotte and went to her little room. Charlotte's family history always caused her anxiety. The fact the chief of police knew about Charlotte's criminal activities. That made Prudence wonder how many bad things people ignored for their own good. It was hard to blame Charlotte when Prudence knew the reason for all of that was her problems.

Prudence started working. She paid close attention to everyone who came in. Most came to see her, and some even stroked up conversations. Prudence found it comforting some didn't know why Charlotte was so upset before. Some were confused, some were annoyed, but no one probed deeper.

Prudence, however, used her position as the amnesiac to get them to come as close to her as possible. She braced herself for adverse reactions and focused on figuring out if they were human or not. It was the least she could do.

It caused some awkwardness when the young man that brought her coffee yesterday seemed to think she was flirting and asked her out. Luckily that was when Charlotte came in through the door. Prudence didn't have to come up with an excuse that didn't confirm his assumption.

"John, don't hit on my cousin. I will smack ya."

"Okay, okay." John grinned, leaving the room with his hand running through his long blond hair.

Charlotte watched him go. "Well, ya could do worse. He takes hints very well and is not a jerk. Just don't eat him."

"I was checking to see if he was human or not." Prudence got up from her chair. She had stopped trying to decipher Charlotte's sarcastic phrases. She could not think about relationships now, though it was tempting to seek comfort for herself in someone. "Trying to figure out if there is someone we need to watch out for."

"Well, I can help ya with that later. Now we need to go to the doctor." Charlotte handed Prudence her jacket.

"You mean go to the person you were talking to on the phone yesterday?" Prudence put her jacket on.

"Yup. His name is Philip, and he works in the hospital in town. And he'll be just the thing to make your illness credible."

The drive to the hospital was long considering how short the distance seemed to Prudence. It was in the busy part of town with the tall buildings.

Inside there was the hustle and bustle of a busy day and the strange smell that nearly made Prudence gag. She could smell blood and metal underneath the overpowering smell. The blood seemed different kinds of off. She assumed it was because the people here were sick. She hoped she wouldn't catch anything. Though she was surprised and glad about the diversity in the place.

They walked straight into the doctor's office, bypassing everyone. Philip was a tall, broad-shouldered man with short brown hair. He was reading something on the computer and straightened up immediately when he saw Charlotte walk in. He did not wait for Charlotte to get near him, he closed the distance and hugged her close to him. Prudence felt her cheeks heat up when Charlotte wrapped her hands around Philips's head and gave him a long deep kiss. Prudence looked away, but she could not shut off all of her senses. She could hear their hearts speeding up and practically feel the atmosphere in the room. She wondered if she should step away when Charlotte and Philip broke their embrace.

"Hey." His voice was soft and warm. Prudence was now certain her guess was right. Charlotte and this man were involved. She was curious to see which types of relationships were prevalent these days. People did seem to have no problem with public displays of intimacy, a fact that Prudence did not know how to feel about.

“Hey, ya.” Charlotte leaned on the desk, her gaze making sure they were alone. “This is my cousin. I need ya to examine her and write a teensy little fib in her file. Well, two teensy little fibs.”

“What type of ‘fibs’?” He raised his left eyebrow.

“The date for one. A week before today. And two, I need ya to write in that she still hasn’t recovered from her car crash fully. She has retrograde amnesia from it, but her body has healed already. Oh, and I’ll bring ya all the documentation ya’ll need to make the report tomorrow. She doesn’t have access to them today.”

“You’ll owe me.”

“Aware of that. But I like owing ya.”

The man smiled. “Okay, done. Let me perform a rudimentary examination.”

Prudence resisted raising an eyebrow. She observed the man carefully. She concluded Charlotte was probably the only person who could get away with asking something like that.

Charlotte nodded and turned to Prudence. “He’ll examine ya to see if ya’re healthy. I’ll stay right here.”

Prudence nodded and walked to the man. He was now exuding polite professionalism.

“My name is Doctor Wentworth. I’ll just perform some rudimentary tests, alright? What’s your name?”

"Prudence." Prudence made an effort to sound vulnerable. She lowered her voice and glanced toward Charlotte more than she looked at the doctor. Charlotte nodded in sympathy if he looked her way, but otherwise smirked.

The doctor used a device that looked like the headphones a cop wore to listen to music while typing up reports, with a flat round end to listen to her heartbeat.

"Wow, that's loud and fast." He commented before wrapping her arm in a strange cloth band. "This will measure your blood pressure."

He squeezed a little round ball, and the band tightened, pressing the flat end of the headphones into Prudence's flesh. The doctor stared at a metal round clock-like thing, whose arrow moved up with every squeeze. When he slowly started turning a knob on the ball he was squeezing, the band released, and the arrow dropped.

"Blood pressure on the high side of normal."

He then checked her mobility. He asked her what her injuries were and where they were located. Prudence turned to Charlotte.

"She doesn't really remember, but she had a concussion, some light whiplash, and a few impact injuries. The airbag absorbed most of the hit, and she would've been fine if she didn't hit her head on something."

"Well, you seem to be fine now. Let me check something else." He flashed a light in her eyes, making them water.

"Response normal. How is your memory?"

"I remember little from before three days ago." Prudence looked at Charlotte, who nodded. "And what I do is fuzzy."

"You probably just need time." The doctor turned to Charlotte. "I assume you did a complete exam at home?"

"Yup." Charlotte lied.

Dr. Wentworth started writing something down on a notepad. "Okay then, I'll put this on hold and then slip it through when you get me her info." He seemed to be used to discussing things with Charlotte like this because as soon as he wrote down what he needed to, he added, "How about Saturday at seven?"

"Make it eight. I'll pick ya up." Charlotte grabbed Prudence by the hand. "See ya." She gave Dr. Wentworth a quick peck on the cheek before leaving.

On the drive back, Prudence couldn't help but ask. "So how did you manage to be in this… relationship?"

"Well, we had an official thing a while back, before I left for school. Then it turned into an unofficial thing when I got back. We see each other when one of us has an excuse, either a real or an imaginary one. We have dinner, end up at one of our homes, knock boots, and in the morning, we have breakfast. Works for me, especially since we mesh well in that department." Charlotte turned to gauge Prudence's reaction. "Ya don't seem fazed."

"Why would I be? That is not a new thing. I think you assume people from the past didn't have any experiences like that, at least it looks like that from the things I've read."

Prudence looked at the road. “In fact, that type of relationship sounds familiar to me.” She didn’t mention her thoughts about the man immediately accepting Charlotte’s request. “I don’t know why it would be, but then I don’t know who I was. Maybe I was not ready to settle down either. Or maybe whoever I was with wasn’t.”

" Maybe that tall dark and maybe handsome man that put ya to sleep is one. That way, when you find him, if he’s alive, you can ask him what type of person you were. Maybe he can jog your memory.” Charlotte teased.

"Maybe I'll find out. If he or anyone else is alive, that is. I have a feeling they aren’t."

“God knows ya could use someone to help you deal with all of this. So, ya think you’re well enough to do that? Have a relationship I mean. Even if it’s just a physical one that will take your mind off your problems for a few hours a week.”

“I do not know, honestly. I am too busy trying to figure out who I am to think about it. I think I need to settle that before I jump into a relationship with someone, no matter how brief. Plus, I need to figure out what feeling is because I want to feed off of someone and which one is because I am attracted to them.” Prudence thought of all the times she had focused on someone’s heartbeat.

“Well, honestly we’ve all had that dilemma. Do I want to sleep with them, or do I want to kill them? Usually, it leads to angry sex and a hoarse throat from shouting." Charlotte laughed. "Ya'll be fine, that's normal."

"That actually makes me feel better. Though I still need to be careful; I am, after all, stronger than a human. I don't want that to lead to accidents."

"You're good at controlling yourself, I've seen it."

"The first time you met me I had eaten 3 people."

"Because ya hadn't eaten in four hundred years. Ya didn't kill me. I am sure that when it's someone ya care about, it will be even harder to kill them."

"I sure hope you're right about that." Prudence closed her eyes as Charlotte drove back to work.

When inside Charlotte went with Prudence to her office and poured out the contents of her purse. It seemed Charlotte had copied everything she got her hands on.

"We need to pour over this and find a clue."

"I have time; I can do it." Prudence gathered all the papers in one empty folder she found while working. It had the name Mackenzie on it. "This might throw people off no?"

"Yeah, maybe. Just don't lose them."

Prudence opened the thin drawer in the desk. It was empty aside from a pen and dust. "I'll put it here when not working on it."

"Wow, that drawer has been stuck for ages." Charlotte turned to look at it.

"I just wiggled it a bit, and it opened. But no one else

will think to try. And I can make it stick again by just hitting it here really hard." Prudence pointed on the underside of the desk.

“Good thinking.” Charlotte straightened up. “Now I have to go and pretend to be my usual self.”

When Charlotte left, Prudence started on the file. The first thing she did was put the papers in order by date and contents. Then she was left with four piles, each for a different identity. Joe Harris, Alexander Barneson, Grant Drayton, and Lens Mills. After repeating several times that she wasn’t going to take any of the things she read to heart, she read through each one.

Joe Harris was the one she started with. A few burglaries, and aggravated assault. Then an attempted murder in another state. The next few years were quiet until the police started chasing him again, this time for three murders, deemed accidental after a few months.

Alexander Barneson had a longer list. From what Prudence could understand, he was suspected to be an assassin for hire, since he only killed rather rich targets. This was the identity with the five counts of murder, one of which involved three people. He was arrested twice. But once he somehow mysteriously vanished from his cell, and the other time, a very expensive lawyer came in and freed him, giving him an alibi.

Prudence might have been new to this world, but she wasn't unfamiliar with the fact money could move a lot of mountains and open a lot of locked doors. She also saw the note a cop had left in the file. It said that if one dug deep enough and weren't being 'stonewalled,' an expression Prudence could guess the meaning of within the context, they would be able to connect the man with a lot more cases.

Grant Drayton was what she assumed to be the man's real identity. Mostly because his file had the most information, and shared a last name with the woman whose file was now missing. Grant was an only child, left in front of a church. Of course, he was, Prudence thought as she shuddered at the image of the tattoos on the man's body. He had been in contact with the police steadily over the years. The first time being when he witnessed a murder but couldn't identify the man responsible. As Prudence read the report, she was becoming surer and surer that the kid was there to learn and not just as an accidental witness. And that the holy man who had died was the murderer who failed at his job. The case had been closed since there was no evidence, and all the child had said was that it was a tall man dressed in black, trying to get money.

As the years went on, it seemed like Grant had fallen on hard times because of his experience, but Prudence saw skills being honed. While she didn't quite understand the process of collecting the evidence and the way certain things were done, the end results were easy enough to understand and compare. Especially when looking at stabbings with wood shavings in the wound or being lit on fire. One beheading. What they all had in common was that the reports about the bodies were extremely scarce compared to a lot of other cases Prudence had read. She even pulled out a case from the same year and compared them. Any report connected to Grant Drayton left a lot to be desired.

Lens Mills was the identity the man used in this town. Prudence could see why. Lens had a few parking tickets, and an assault charge that was ruled as self-defense, but no heavy crimes. Prudence was wondering how the man kept his identities straight. It seemed that if he didn't use the correct disguise and remembered the name wrong, he would be toast immediately. When one compared the pictures of the four identities, three had different hair lengths, and two had different eye colors. All had completely different information when it came to a place of birth, age, and current residence. Well, to be fair, only one had a current residence. An apartment in Delaware. Prudence wrote the address down, hoping that she might be able to poke around somewhere.

At this point, she hadn’t realized how much time had passed. Then she looked at the clock above the door and saw that she had been studying the file for over three hours. She packed everything up and placed it neatly in the drawer, then took the piece of paper with the address and went to Charlotte.

“Well, we need to be careful how we search for this. We

don’t want those guys in suits again.” Charlotte stared at the paper.

“What if I just search for news about Delaware at first?” Prudence was trying hard to picture the internet in her head. But invisible strings that somehow pulled data out of nowhere was not something she could understand. Though ‘the black box is the modern filing cabinet’ was easier.

“Well, yeah it might work. It’s not a stretch to think that if it was in those files, those guys know about it too. And if they were serious about cleaning things up, they’d do something about the apartment.”

“Now, I just need to figure out where to search from and how to do it. Can’t you do it?” Prudence asked Charlotte.

“Ya need to get used to stuff like this more than I do. Computers are pretty much the default equipment everyone uses. Maybe ya can ask someone under the pretense of your amnesia? John doesn’t know enough to contest ya on that, he was not involved in the case, and he’d pretty much do anything if ya ask him.” Charlotte snickered.

“And you’re alright with me using your friend like that?”

"He's not a good friend; he's just a friend. There's a difference. Plus, ya are good at pretending to be something ya're not. Not surprising since ya've done it a lot. Maybe if ya do it often enough, your memory will get jogged. It did happen with the vampire hunter dude."

Prudence's mind latched onto that idea, and with that in mind, she walked over to John near the end of his shift. She walked over to him, as he was throwing things in a backpack and got his attention with a wave.

“Hi, John.”

“Hey, Prue. You mind if I call you that? Or do you prefer your full name?” John beamed at her.

“Either is fine.” Prudence smiled in return. It was odd how calming John’s presence was. She assumed that was because of his posture and the fact he was not threatening at all. “I actually wanted to ask you something.”

“Yes?” He dropped the backpack down and leaned on his desk.

"Well, as you know, I have a case of amnesia, and unfortunately that means I have forgotten quite a few things I knew how to do before. Case in point, using a computer. Just drawing a complete blank." Prudence looked down. She didn't need to pretend she was embarrassed. She already was.

“Hey, that’s okay.” John jumped at the chance to make her feel better. “You want me to teach you?”

“Yes, and I was wondering if you could help me search for something. My cousin tried, but Charlotte gets frustrated easily.”

“Sure, anything in particular?”

“Well, I had a friend in Delaware, but I can’t seem to find her address or name. The doctor said if I see enough things that are familiar to me it might jog my memory.”

Prudence wondered how she thought of that as fast as she did.

“Sure, sit down.” John pulled out his chair for her. Prudence felt flattered by the gesture. “Alright, you see this button,” he pointed at a large square on the black box under the desk, “this turns it on. Push it.”

Prudence turned on the computer. She was pleasantly surprised at the practicality of John's explanations. He put a hand on the back of the chair she was sitting on and pointed with his other hand. Prudence was hyper aware of that hand. The closer they were the more Prudence could smell John’s body. It had an oddly sweet note under the aroma of what she assumed was a shower gel. She chose not to focus on it and focused on the screen instead.

"Okay, now this is a keyboard where you type things. This is the mouse. When you move it," John demonstrated, "the little arrow on the screen moves. And when you click this button," John pointed to the left mouse button, "twice, you open stuff. Now, if you were to search for Delaware, you'd first need to open a search engine. Click twice on that little icon." John pointed at the screen with his finger.

Prudence moved the mouse and clicked. The screen changed. She did her best not to seem overly surprised. But she did find John’s explanations easy to digest. He might be worth keeping around.

"Alright, now we click here and type Delaware. Hold the

key that says shift while typing a letter to capitalize it. Then press enter." John's voice was calm and steady.

Prudence did that. The screen changed showing a bunch of general information about the state.

"That thing." John pointed at the end of the screen, "means there is something more down the page, so you use the little wheel to move the page up and down. To scroll."

Prudence tried it, feeling more confident. She noticed that when someone stood this close to her for this long, she could feel their body heat more. She wondered how exactly advanced her senses were. She could also hear the steady beating of his heart. There was a weird warm knot in her stomach. She refused to focus on it, instead staring at the screen.

"Okay, so let's say you want the news to a particular region. You have any idea where your friend was from specifically?" John turned his face toward her. Prudence felt her mouth go dry. That was surely not how one felt when they were hungry, Prudence thought. Her brain was telling her to move, but her body was urging her to move forward. She compromised by staying perfectly still.

"Wilmington," Prudence said after she realized that the pause had become too long. Her heartbeat sped up.

"Okay, so above you type Wilmington and the word news." John moved his glance to the computer screen.

When Prudence typed it up and clicked enter, the page changed. Out of the flurry of information, she focused on a title where it said that a fire had engulfed an apartment building. She wanted to open it, but she didn't want to scare John.

"How can I open two things at once?"

"For that, you need the right button, you click it over the title, and you then click the other button over this option." John pointed at the button, and his hand brushed against hers.

Prudence clicked the thing she was interested in and then another title at random, about a park.

"Okay, now click over."

Prudence clicked the news about the fire and read it quickly. She was unused to reading on a screen, but it didn't bother her too much. She saw the address was the same as the one she wrote down.

"Don't tell me that fire is where your friend lived," John asked. He stopped leaning on the chair and knelt next to Prudence, so he could look her in her eyes. She could tell his pulse sped up. He was worried for her. Prudence suddenly started to feel bad about using him. She decided to not follow her instinct to hug him.

Prudence kept her face neutral but avoided his gaze. She didn't know if it was only because she felt her eyes would give her lie away, or if it had something to do with the knot in her stomach. That knot was spreading. She could not stop focusing on his heartbeat. "I don't know; it doesn't jog anything." After a break that allowed her to read the whole thing, she added, "I don't think so, at least I don't remember it."

She clicked over to the park and after a few moments faked a smile. “Oh, I remember this park. I think I’ve been there.”

"That's great." John's voice sounded relieved, and he got back to his previous position. Prudence guessed that he was worried he had triggered a bad memory. And he had triggered something.

She felt unused to a man standing that close to her, sharing this type of moment with her, while having a beating heart. It was the one thing that was off, though it wasn’t enough for it to feel alien. Hearing his heartbeat made her remember her mission. But apart from that, the strange feeling was familiar. Warm. She read the article to its end, and even clicked on some pictures, making up a memory of sitting on a bench.

When she got up to go, John lightly grabbed her hand. “Hey, about my question this morning…”

Prudence could feel his pulse through his wrist. He was now closer to her, his body just a hair away from hers. For a moment she tried to double check if it was her vampire instincts taking over, but she didn’t feel hungry. The knot in her stomach became bigger and her face flushed. She imagined what would happen if she had actually said yes. Maybe kissed him. It brought butterflies to her stomach. And then a cold chill went down her spine. She couldn’t. She wasn’t human; she was a monster that fed on them. She couldn't trust herself with him. She did not want to hurt anyone. So, she automatically said the first thing that she thought of, omitting the vampire part.

"It was sweet. And I might have said yes, but I feel that right now, with my brain the way it is, I can't dedicate any time to things like that, even in a casual form. You understand what I mean?"

John smiled. "Yeah, I do. So, how about, we stay friends for now? And when you feel better, if I'm single and you don't discover you have a partner waiting for you somewhere, we can give this a try?" He was still close to her, but now he started to back away. She let go of his wrist.

"Sure, I'd like that." Prudence tried to smile, but just as her lips moved, she felt her fangs had started extending. She quickly closed her mouth. It might have been too quick because one of her fangs scraped the inside of her mouth and lower gums. Prudence's eyes widened. She quickly swallowed whatever blood she had in her mouth. The blood was a faint mix of sour and bitter.

"Well, if you need help again ask." John put his hands in his pocket. "Bye."

Prudence knew she couldn't open her mouth. The panic overwhelmed her, and she no longer thought of the fuzzy feelings in her stomach. Her fangs were not retracting. She wanted to run away. In her frantic search, she saw a stack of napkins on John's table. She grabbed one and covered her mouth and nose with it.

“Sorry, I think I have a cold.” She mumbled through the napkin, hoping blood didn’t drip anywhere.

John nodded, walking even further away, but his posture was still relaxed, and he didn’t seem offended. “That’s okay.”

“Bye.” Prudence turned and headed for the door.

Charlotte, who was already in the car waiting, raised her eyebrows when Prudence got inside and sighed. That was when her fangs retracted up into her gums.

“Do I need to be worried?” Charlotte seemed to be smirking. “Did ya eat him? Do I need to go and get the first aid kit?”

“No, he’s fine. But I need to learn how to control these things. I almost blew it.” Prudence allowed herself to laugh and be pleased with how well she handled it despite the problem.

After a short recap, Charlotte lit a cigarette. “So, they torched the place. Figures. Also, good job on the park idea. I used to think ya were good at pretending because ya had to hide the vampireness, but now I think ya were a calculating woman. Also, no you’re not too big of a monster to be in a relationship, or even knock boots with someone.”

“Thanks.” Prudence smiled. While it did make her feel better, she didn’t believe Charlotte’s words. “What about the heartbeat thing?”

“Well, we knew the guy that brought you here was a vampire, so maybe ya grew up in that world? Maybe ya saw humans as snacks.”

“I don’t feel that way about you. Or Milo, which I am glad about. And I don’t think I feel that way about John.”

“Well, we didn’t flirt with you. And I have seen the way ya look at people, so ya’re definitely into guys. Only maybe they need to be undead for you not to feel weird about being with them. I am certain that ya didn’t stay a virgin for all of that time. Ya are a creature of the night; ya don’t follow our dumb rules. I bet you had all kinds of wonderful, toe curling experiences.”

“Which I do not remember. So, it’s the same as if I never had those experiences. All I have is a vague feeling that I have experienced something like that before.” Prudence thought back at her familiarity with flirting. She shook her head to stop thinking about it and focused on Charlotte's cigarette. "You know, you said you smoke, but this is only the second or third time I've seen you with a cigarette. You smoke one and then stop. That's the same package you had a few days ago."

“I smoke when I’m stressed. And I smoked two on the balcony yesterday after we came home.” Charlotte blew the smoke out of the window. “I prefer destroying my lungs over drinking myself into a stupor and losing a few brain cells.”

“And this impairs you far less in the short run.” Prudence imagined Charlotte facing a vampire hunter drunk. It was over pretty quickly and not the least bit funny. She did not know how she would feel if someone she knew got hurt.

“Tomorrow I don’t have work. So, I’ll go get your IDs, finish some errands, and I’ll then take what the good doctor needs to the hospital, then take him out. Means ya can do whatever you want tomorrow.”

"I think I'll walk around town a bit." Prudence was not only feeling cramped; she felt bored. She knew the sun didn't really bother her if she wore a hat and long sleeves, so walking around would be perfectly fine. While she didn’t mind spending time alone or with Milo, she wanted to see what the town had to offer.

“Sure, I’ll leave ya some money, and explain the currency. I know ya must hate being at home all the time. I know I do. Just don’t come and say hi if ya see me and the doc.” Charlotte pulled into the driveway.

“I am perfectly capable of not ruining a dinner. And whatever that dinner leads to.” Prudence got out of the car.

Milo had been cooking again. This time, Prudence sat down and ate immediately. The food didn’t nourish her nearly as much as blood did, but it filled a need blood never could.

She ignored the spicy sauce in the bowl on the table, while Charlotte took it and liberally poured it over her food. Prudence figured that if her scent and sight were better than a human’s, maybe her taste buds were too. She didn’t want to overwhelm herself.

After the dinner, Milo heard the explanation for Charlotte's phone call.

"There hasn't been anything off here, and maybe there won't be, but I'll be careful either way." He shrugged.

"I'm not risking anyone. If this whole conspiracy exists, then the people who killed off everyone else in our family are the same people who now know we're here." Charlotte lit another cigarette.

Milo turned and studied Prudence's face. She knitted her eyebrows, unable to decipher his expression.

"Anything you want to say, Milo?" She asked him directly. She quickly dismissed the idea he was angry at her because he did not look it.

"I don't want you to feel like you're the reason this is happening." Milo reached over and held Prudence's hand. She found the warmth comforting.

"I'm not. According to what we know, I didn't really have a choice in the matter." Prudence shrugged. "If we were to blame anyone, I would more turn to the man who brought me here or the ones after me."

Charlotte smirked. "She's not like ya Milo."

Milo rolled his eyes at Charlotte. "It's normal for people to feel bad even if it's not their fault. You focus on the case; I focus on other things, like making sure our new friend doesn't feel bad about herself."

"I appreciate it anyway." Prudence squeezed his hand in return. Deep inside she was happy he cared enough to say it.

Milo and Charlotte soon retreated to their rooms. Prudence didn't really understand what Milo specifically did, but she knew it involved a lot of books, reading, and writing. He was hunched over on his bed, his floor and sheets covered with paper, books, and pens. He looked really peaceful and almost beautiful like that, she thought. He seemed to be right at home and at peace, his breathing was steady. His face was furrowed in concentration. Prudence had never really seen someone concentrate that much on something.

She didn't really like standing to the side and observing people, it felt too odd, so she investigated the rest of the rooms.

Charlotte was asleep in her bed, on her stomach, face full of a pillow, her covers and sheets bunched around as if she had a fight in the bed. Prudence quickly closed the door, not wanting to wake Charlotte.

The other rooms have not been touched since their occupants died. Which meant everything was in the same place, and there was a thick layer of dust everywhere. She could tell which rooms belonged to older people, and which to younger ones.

She opened drawers, rummaged through notebooks and diaries, but didn't find anything too interesting. There was nothing about her, even in Uncle Tim's room. There were date books and diaries with random details about their life. And while the visits to the graveyard were mentioned, nothing else was. Prudence was amazed at the level of secrecy.

In a few rooms, she found ledgers with payments and names, which she assumed was the only thing showing the family's criminal past. She couldn't understand what the acronyms meant, or if the different pen colors meant different things, or if the person lost their pens a lot.

There were various weapons as well. There was a whole cabinet filled with rifles and guns. In a drawer she found knives.

Prudence stopped and thought of how the vampire hunter had caught her off guard. After a few seconds of thought, she picked a small switchblade out of the bunch. After checking she knew how to use it, and that it was sharp, she put it in her pants pocket. While she wasn't sure she was ever going to use it, the fact it was there made her feel safer. And she didn't really want Milo or Charlotte to have to save her all the time.

When she made her way down the stairs, she stopped at a cabinet. It was light and reminded her of the one in her dream. She opened it. The inside had a bunch of old photos of the Davenports. She picked up album by album, and envelope after envelope, looking through them but didn't recognize anyone. No photographs of the time she came here would exist, so she didn't bother looking for the man that brought her here. Though she did find a photo of the woman whose grave she was in and whose name she was using.

That Prudence couldn't be more different. She had a round smiley face and light hair. She seemed nice and cheery. Her smile lit up all the other faces around her. As the photos went on, that Prudence aged but never lost her light. The vampire Prudence looked at the photos with an expression of longing. The smile reminded her of things she might never have. She didn't know if she aged. And the prospect of living forever, watching everything around you age and break apart suddenly seemed like a very real possibility. She didn't know if she could handle losing people she cared about, even if they have lived a full life.

She started wondering if she had anyone out there that cared for her. Was she a product of a banned romance, or something more twisted? Was she unwanted? Or did her parents spend their nights guarding her? Was her mother a vampire, or her father? Is one of them still alive? If they are, would they cheer her hunters on, or try and stop them?

She put the photos back and focused on the feelings cropping up in her head, trying to see if they would jog something. She wished she could remember why that man had put her to sleep, leaving her alone. And did he actually plan on coming back and explaining himself, or did he lie? Or was he already dead? If she had her memories, would she feel sad about it? Did the person Prudence was before care about that man?

Prudence hugged her knees and watched the sunrise. Later, she went downstairs for her daily dose of blood.

CHAPTER TWENTY-SIX

Milo had woken up first. Prudence found him in the kitchen.

"Want breakfast?" He smiled at her. Prudence nodded. He gave her what he said was toast and a cup of coffee, and then watched her carefully as she heated up her blood in the microwave. Prudence noticed how softly he always observed her. It was something she couldn't fathom. Didn't he know she was a monster that fed on his kind?

"You're catching up quickly." He beamed at her. Prudence felt better.

Prudence hadn't tried coffee before, but considering Milo and Charlotte had it every morning, she could guess what it did.

"I drink it with a lot of milk, while Charlotte adds a lot of sugar. Try and see how you like it."

Prudence decided to try drinking it plain then adding milk, then sugar. She didn't like it at all, but she did find it gave her a lot of energy. She finally realized how Milo could sleep so little and still function.

Charlotte came in and scarfed down the food without blinking. "I'll be leaving right away because I want to kick our little friend's butt into gear. Plus, I'm excited about getting everything I need to do done."

Prudence didn't really pay attention to the rush. She slowly got ready, putting on clothes she assumed would be comfortable in all day, which wound up being a long dress. She brushed her hair and put on a floppy hat. She liked her freedom of choosing whatever she wanted to wear. She picked up a jacket and some shoes by the door.

Charlotte gave her a wallet with money, writing down the currencies. Prudence found she didn't need a lot of time to remember them. After the first time she saw them they were engraved in her mind.

"What do ya want to do? There is a museum, and a movie theater, and a lot of shops and some restaurants, but not a lot else." Charlotte was running a brush through her hair.

"I'll see. I have all day." Prudence shrugged.

"Okay… well, here." Charlotte gave Prudence a cell phone. "This is an old phone I had. If ya want to call me, just press and hold the number two button until the thing starts ringing. If ya want to call Milo, press the number three button the same way. Then put it to your ear and talk." Charlotte mimicked a phone call.

"I understand, thanks. But I don't know where to put all these things."

"Here." Charlotte gave Prudence a smaller brown bag hanging on a hook. "Just toss anything in there. I'll ring ya, to give ya your ID so that ya can go anywhere."

"Thank you." Prudence gave Charlotte a smile.

Outside, it was loud and crowded. Prudence navigated the street. It looked filled with people, but considering she knew the town held around 500,000 residents, she would bet it was a slow day. She walked along the street, trying to figure out which building and store were for what just by glance. The more she walked, the more it seemed she understood the way the world worked better. The way people whizzed around fast but stopped to greet everyone anyway. People rarely bumped into her, but when they did, they apologized. One of those people was an old man. Prudence was certain he couldn't see very well, and he tipped his hat to her after she helped him with his dropped grocery bag and his cane.

She stopped at a store that had a pair of shears on the window, with a silhouette of a woman's face. She had just come close to it when an older woman came out of there and started talking.

"Hello, dear are you here for an appointment?" The woman seemed very excited.

When Prudence shook her head, the woman waved it off. "No matter, I got a cancellation, and I know you're Charlotte's cousin, and that makes you an important client." The woman linked her arm to Prudence's and dragged her into the store.

"I'm Gladys, and oh dear, I can't imagine how you must feel, having that horrible experience. Well, I know just the thing to help. A little pampering never hurts, and always calms the nerves. Let's see if we can make that hair of yours easier to manage and beautiful to boot."

Prudence was intrigued by the woman's energy, so she let her do whatever she wanted. Gladys washed Prudence's hair, which Prudence found very relaxing and then sat Prudence in a chair facing a large mirror. Prudence sat there as Gladys described what she was going to do. She also paid attention to a gaggle of women in the back of the store, their hair wrapped in foil, talking about rumors in the town.

"I heard they thought it was a mugging gone wrong."

"But what mugger needs a cop uniform?"

"I still think it's some kids being dragged into one of those fads, trying to break into places and mess with things. I swear people have gone crazy."

"Well, we won't know. The government picked it up."

"Good, maybe they'll find out what is it really, and stop it."

“Or maybe just cover it up.”

“Oh, please Muriel.”

"What? I watch those television shows; I know how government types can be. Who cares about a few deaths in a tiny little town?"

“Well, he was definitely not a local.”

“Maybe whoever it was left.”

One of the women saw her and nudged the others. Prudence was glad she had been staring directly in front of her instead of at them. The women started whispering, and Prudence thanked her advanced hearing again.

“That girl there… she’s the new Davenport isn’t she?”

“Oh, poor dear, she doesn’t know who she is, doesn't she?”

“You can never trust what that family says.”

"Oh, who would lie about that? Plus, my niece saw her in the hospital. It seems she had a car accident."

“Poor thing. I wonder which side she’s from. She doesn’t look a lot like the boy or girl, and I haven’t seen her before.”

“I bet she’s from Charlotte’s father’s side. There are a lot of people on that side who hadn’t been seen here a long time. And a lot of them traveled abroad.”

“I wonder if her crash had anything to do with all the deaths.”

“Don’t start again with the curse talk, Muriel.”

“You don’t find it odd? So many Davenports dead and this young woman in a car accident.”

“It’s not a curse. Their past caught up with them, and their spawn covered it up.”

“Oh, the young Davenports can’t cover up so many deaths. Plus, she was the one pushing for a bigger investigation. My son said so. There were screaming matches.” Prudence struggled not to react at the memory of Charlotte reacting to the news.

“What about that young man?”

“He’s the nice one. Polite, never hurt a fly, only spending time with his books. He tutored my daughter. His mother raised him well. He didn’t even know about his family reputation. He’d never do it.” Prudence raised her eyebrow, trying to not move because Gladys had scissors. She never knew that Milo didn’t know about the bad things. She wondered if he felt the same way she did when she found out what she was. Yes, he didn’t do anything, unlike Prudence, but it must have been hard. Was that why he was so comfortable with her?

“Plus, the girl is the one with the knowledge.”

"I still think it's a curse. They have so much bad karma; it's bound to come back at them."

“Oh, speaking of that, did you hear, the Smith boy found out his wife was going at it with the handyman.”

Prudence stopped listening when the conversation turned. She focused on Gladys and how the light shined off her silver hair.

Soon, Prudence had hair which moved a lot more, with

what Gladys called long side bangs on the left side of her face, coming down to her jaw. There were soft waves in her hair, which made the hat on her head look a lot better. Her hair length was a little below her collarbones. Prudence didn't think a simple haircut could make her feel that much better, but she felt like a new person. The last traces from her time in the mausoleum have been erased. She wondered if Milo and Charlotte would like it. And if anyone that knew her would recognize her.

Prudence paid and thanked Gladys. "Can you tell me where the library is? I forget."

After Gladys had given her directions, Prudence went to the library. She immediately found a spare computer and sat down. Using what she learned from John at the police station, she typed the name of the town she was in and added history afterward. Prudence scrolled down the articles. She wanted to know exactly when the town was founded. While she typed, she couldn't help thinking about the feeling she had while John taught her. Maybe, if or when she was safe, she could take him up on his offer. Prudence stopped herself from thinking about it now. She needed to focus.

A few long hours later Prudence felt her eyes stinging from staring at the screen. Aside from a young man who was insistent on making a conversation out of asking her questions about what she was researching, no one bothered her.

Prudence got up and moved through the shelves, looking

for books and reading passages when her phone rang. She apologized to the strict-looking librarian and went outside.

"Where are you?" Charlotte's voice rang out.

"Library."

"I'll be there in five minutes to give ya what ya need."

"Sure."

Charlotte approved of the change. "Ya look awesome. Gladys did a great job."

"She did. I also heard something." When Prudence explained what she heard Charlotte laughed.

"Those old gossips. That's pretty much what I expect of them."

"I'm glad. I didn't." Prudence admitted. She wasn't that surprised information spread fast. But hearing someone talking about her friend like that was unsettling.

"Is it true that Milo didn't know about the… things your family did?"

"His mother was insistent that he go to college and get out of here. He was the one that made sure I was left alone when I said I was going to medical school. And then he moved here so I wouldn't be alone."

"That sounds sweet."

"He is a sweet guy. I sometimes feel like he is the only one that always cared about me." Charlotte had a vague smile on her face. Prudence could tell she remembered something.

"Eh, people still assume the worst. Ignore them. But it's

nice to know what the whole town knows." Charlotte hugged Prudence goodbye.

Prudence came back. After acquiring a library card, she took four books with her, to the surprise of the librarian. She stuffed them in her bag then looked for a place she could sit down and read. That turned out to be a coffee shop. The sun wasn't that strong due to the cloudy weather. Prudence could remove her hat and the sweater she was wearing over her short-sleeved dress. She ordered some tea and a scone but found herself engrossed in the book.

"You seem to be having a nice day. Has the cold passed?"

The voice was familiar. Prudence lifted her head and came face to face with John. He was regular clothes, and his hair was in a ponytail. "It's on its way out. It's nice to be able to move around like this. Are you having a nice day?"

"I will if I can join you." The sentence would have been flirting if John's expression wasn't so tame.

Prudence was glad he seemed to be respecting her decision. "Sure, I could use the company of a friend."

John sat down, ordering a coffee. "I like your hair."

"Thanks." Prudence ruffled it.

"What are you reading?"

"Oh, it's historical fiction. I like books, but I haven't had the chance to read in a long while." Prudence assumed she liked books. When she was in the library, she liked leafing through them.

"I don't read much either, but they can be fun. I assume jumping in a familiar hobby would make it easier."

"Well," Prudence took a deep breath. She didn't know why she would share this with him. But she wanted to talk to someone who knew her only as an amnesiac and not as an amnesiac who had killed two people. And who knows how many more. "I'm in a strange city, and all I can remember is facts from the sixteen hundreds, from my classes apparently." Prudence put the book down.

"That would be confusing. You're basically time traveling." John laughed. "But I guess Milo and Charlotte helped."

"Being around people does. I can navigate around and, even if I don't remember anything, I can learn how to function again."

"If you don't mind me asking what happened to you?" John took a sip of his coffee.

"Car accident. I had been in a taxi and apparently hit my head quite severely." Prudence remembered she and Charlotte agreed not to get her a driver's license since she didn't know how to drive. It was easy reciting the story. "I'm almost fully healed, aside from my memory anyway."

"Well, this is a nice place to heal. I like this city."

"I do too." Prudence looked around. "I like that I can experience it for the first time now."

"I assume you have a lot of people calling you, asking you how you are."

"Well, some." Prudence lied. "Being a student doesn't really leave a lot of time for socializing."

"Student?"

"Yes, I've been getting my Masters in History, specializing in the colonization of the US."

"Wow, I'm impressed."

Prudence smiled. "Thanks." She took a sip of her tea and a bite from her scone. This felt like more than a coffee. She found out she didn't mind it.

"Oh, I think the museum has an exhibit about that today." John tapped his fingers on the table, trying to remember. "Yeah, I think that was this week."

"That's wonderful. I was wondering what to do with the rest of my day."

"Plus, it might jog something."

"Yup. What are you doing today?"

"Oh, I need to pick up my sister's kid from practice and then we're going to the port. Otherwise, I'd join you." Prudence noticed how John's smile widened when he talked about the child.

"That's okay. How old is your… nephew?"

"Niece. She's eleven, and she wants to be a police officer. Or a marine biologist. I think. That was last week, though. She might have changed her mind now." He laughed.

"Children are like that. She sounds wonderful." Prudence

wondered if she had any children out there. If she could even have them. Was she even the type to want a family?

"Yeah." John pulled out a photo from his back pocket, showing a little blonde girl in pigtails.

"She's beautiful."

After a few more minutes of chit-chat, enough for Prudence to finish her scone and tea, she left John in the coffee shop with a warm goodbye. He remained at the coffee table, to finish his coffee. Prudence released a relieved breath that her fangs didn't extend this time, even when he got up to hug her. His heartbeat was faster than Milo's or Charlotte, even when the latter one yelled her head off. His body temperature also seemed higher. She didn't know if it was her or him.

She checked the shops on her way to the museum. She only bought things she felt uncomfortable borrowing, so it meant she visited the lingerie store and left with two bags.

The museum did have an exhibit about the Colonial era, which she was glad about. There was a lot of art, so Prudence got to see her world. Some of the pictures were evoking familiar feelings, no matter how painful. No memories, though. She was going to be sad about that, but then she realized that if she had a memory flash right now, she would feel a lot of pain. And curling up in a ball in such a public place was not something she could do. As she was walking around with a vague smile on her face, a picture made her stop.

The photo was a group portrait, lovingly painted and probably restored several times. There were four women and five men, all dressed in finery. Prudence focused on a man in the back right.

He looked tall, at least taller than everyone else, with dark hair falling over his equally dark eyes. His skin was pale, and he looked younger than his expression. He had chiseled features, a strong jaw, and a long narrow nose which fit with what appeared to be a very lanky body. Prudence felt she knew him. But also, she felt her heart speed up. Whether it was because of fear or excitement, she didn't know.

She spent a long time studying the photo. The building they were in front of was a hospital that had stopped existing a while back. She felt like it wasn't really as important or recognizable to her. Most of the others in the photo felt human, aside from a lady with ashen hair and brown eyes too big for her round face and a stocky old man who stood weirdly, like he was used to there being more of him. Prudence didn't want to jump to conclusions about those two, but something in her head told her the dark-haired man was the vampire who brought her here.

The other two women were both brown haired and solemn. They looked like sisters. The three men looked very different from one another. One was short and pudgy the second was a bit taller but wider still while the third almost blended in with the background. The man Prudence assumed to be a vampire stood out too much, and despite the seriousness of his expression, he seemed to be the one happiest to be here.

Prudence scanned the plaque under it for names. She connected all the people from left to right, but when she came to the man, all it said was ‘unknown.'

“Damn,” she muttered. None of the other names felt familiar either.

“You’re looking for something?” An old man Prudence guessed to be the one in charge of the exhibit approached her. He was short, balding, with a red and white plaid suit and a black bowtie.

“Oh, I was just curious about this picture, specifically this man.” Prudence pointed at the picture.

“Oh, yes that man is interesting. I have cataloged every photo here extensively, and more even, but I have never managed to find his name in a record, and he shows up in pictures years apart. Odd.” The old man looked up hopefully at Prudence. “Want to see?”

“Oh yes, that sounds very interesting.” Prudence smiled widely and nodded. She could see the man’s eyes brighten at the fact someone was interested in what he had to say.

The old man walked her around the exhibit, showing her every photo. The dark-haired man was depicted a lot of times. Sometimes in places where one would think they just used a general looking person as a stand-in. Like a picture depicting people putting out a fire.

"This is 1615; this is 1667. And he looks exactly the same. If this was just a model they used, he got around."

Prudence stood around and acted interested, while inside counting the data she received. The fact he didn't age noticeably convinced her that he was a vampire. He was obviously able to at least pass as white since no one was dismissive of him and he seemed to be the man in charge of things in several depictions. He also spent a lot of time in the New World, helping like a Good Samaritan. He seemed invested in what was going on around him. Could a vampire care about humans like this?

The old man was positively vibrating as Prudence got him to take her in the back, to look through the archives. She found it easy to listen to him and ask questions. He flipped over photos and paintings, showed her all kinds of things and never seemed to slow down, despite the fact he must have been around sixty.

Prudence patiently waited until he was called away. He thought her a nice, meek girl, so he didn't even hesitate to leave her alone for 'just one minute.'

When he left, Prudence immediately rifled through everything as neatly and quietly as possible. She got to a stack of photos from the 1800s and froze when she found him in the background of one. He looked exactly the same, aside from his clothes. He tried to fit in so much he vanished unless you were looking for him.

She couldn't believe it. Pulling out her phone, she

unlocked in and pressed around frantically until she realized where the camera function was. She focused the phone on the photo until it looked clear and pressed the button with the same shape on it as the one on the previous button a few times. Hoping she caught what she wanted, she continued looking.

As she rummaged through the things, the phone still in her hand shivered and rang. Prudence answered.

"Where are ya?" Charlotte's voice was higher than normal, and she sounded agitated. From the outside noise and her heavy breathing Prudence could tell she was running.

“Museum basement.”

“Milo raised the alarm. I’m running as fast as I can, do the same.”

Prudence nodded, then remembered Charlotte couldn’t see her. “I’ll be there.” Prudence nodded and then put her phone in her bag. She had just picked it up when the old man returned.

“Oh, you’re leaving?”

“Trust me I don’t want to.” Prudence extended a hand-shake. “But I was called away and need to hurry. I’ll be back as soon as possible.”

When the man shook her hand, Prudence made her way through the museum then broke into a run. She zigzagged between people, who ducked out of her way.

She focused on the house as she made her way down the

street and through the crowd, retracing her steps. Her speed steadily increased from human to vampire the closer she came to the house, and the fewer people there were in the street.

A sharp scent hit her nostrils. Blood. Prudence's vision tunneled, and her stomach twisted into a knot. When she heard a crash and glass breaking, her blood boiled over. Her feet barely touched the ground as she bolted in the house, up the stairs, and down the hallway, following the sounds. Prudence stopped when she saw Charlotte's back.

Charlotte was standing in the hallway, the gun in her hands pointed at a woman in old tattered clothes and messy short hair. The woman was somehow too tall and too thin for the frame she had, her skin deathly pale. Prudence didn't think anyone could look even more like a vampire, even if they tried. The woman had lifted Milo off his feet and slammed him into the wall. She was trying to both not break the grip she had around his neck, but at the same time remove the metal crucifix he had wedged between his neck and her hand. Her hand was burning, blisters forming all over it.

"Unless you want him dead, you should do as I say. Now, where's the mutt?"

"The fuck ya talking about?" Charlotte deadpanned.

Prudence couldn't believe how calm Charlotte and Milo looked. Prudence felt as if her heart had jumped to her throat.

The vampire stared Charlotte down. "Tell me when 'Prudence,'" she uttered the name with disgust, "is set to meet the one that brought her here and I'll release him. Don't, and he dies."

Prudence sighed. She wasn't sure the vampire was going to do as she said even if Charlotte had the answers.

"And if I don't know?" Charlotte asked.

"Then I have no use for you." The vampire grew claws on her free hand. She moved quicker than Prudence could see, and suddenly Milo was bleeding from a slash in his stomach, and the vampire was throwing him away.

Charlotte didn't even have time to fire. The vampire was already behind her. The vampire grabbed Charlotte's hands and pulled them behind. She was about to sink her fangs into Charlotte's neck.

Prudence saw red. She couldn't let anyone hurt her friends. She ran up behind the vampire and grabbed her by the face. Prudence's hand clamped around the vampire's mouth trying to stop the fangs from extending. Small claws grew over Prudence's nails and dug into the vampire's cheeks.

The vampire's head moved back, hitting Prudence in the face. She then kicked Charlotte away while still holding onto her hand. Prudence was certain everyone heard the sickening crunch Charlotte's shoulder made.

Prudence let the vampire go and reached up to feel her broken nose.

The vampire turned around and swung at Prudence. Prudence ducked, but the vampire's other hand slashed her across the arm.

Prudence grabbed the vampire by the shoulders and drove a knee into her stomach. The vampire laughed, as her free hands slammed into Prudence's sides. Prudence was certain the claws touched bone.

The vampire wrenched her hands away and then attacked with a flurry of blows. She was fast, too fast for Prudence. As Prudence was trying to get the vampire away from Milo and Charlotte, she could feel the blows chipping away at her body. The blows targeted her vital points. Her eye was stinging, and there was blood flowing down her cheeks, arms, and torso. She managed to block a few shots, so her arms were already bruising. Her one punch that landed right on the vampire's jaw barely broke the skin.

The vampire grabbed Prudence by the hair and slammed her face against the wall. Prudence heard gunshots. The vampire shuddered then turned around. Prudence could see Milo, barely standing, manning a rifle, while Charlotte was holding a gun.

The vampire started to turn towards them. Milo and Charlotte continued firing. Whatever the bullets were, they were doing a lot of damage. Prudence could hear the vampire's flesh sizzling.

Prudence focused and brought all her strength down on the vampire's foot. When the vampire released her hair, she shot up, slamming her outstretched hand into the soft part under the jaw. The claws sunk into the flesh.

The vampire turned to hit Prudence, but the gunshots made her shudder. Prudence forced her fingers through the flesh, right into the vampire's mouth.

All Prudence could think right now was how afraid she was for Milo and Charlotte. The vampire in front of her started to sneer when the gunshots stopped. Prudence knew it right then and there. This person in front of her was a monster. One with no regards for life.

Prudence let her fangs grow out. All outside sounds melted away, and all she could hear was her own heartbeat and the sounds coming out of the vampire's sneering mouth. With strength she hadn't unleashed since the ambulance, Prudence closed her hand around the vampire's jaw and yanked.

The jaw disconnected at its weakest point. Flesh ripped, and blood sprayed all around the walls. Prudence dropped the mass of bone on the floor and backhanded the vampire into the wall.

"Go," she said to Milo and Charlotte. They nodded and left as fast as they could, Charlotte applying pressure to Milo's wound as her other hand hung beside her body. They sunk in the first open door.

Gurgling noises Prudence could assume to be laughter rang out, and the vampire was on her feet. Before Prudence knew it, she was on the floor, and the vampire was trying to claw her eyes out. Fangs weren't of much use without a lower jaw, but when they were as large as the ones staring Prudence in the face, they couldn't be ignored.

Prudence stuck her hands up. Claws shredded her arms while a fang was stabbed through her palm. Prudence kicked the vampire between the legs repeatedly, then used her other clawed hand to slash at the vampire’s stomach.

The fang in her hand broke off from the vampire’s mouth. Prudence punched the vampire in the face, feeling the bones in her hand snapping. The vampire flew to the side.

Prudence got up, breathing heavily. Just then she noticed the sun right out of the open window. Behind the vampire.

Before the vampire could fully straighten, Prudence ran towards her and pushed her out of it.

There was a dull bump, and Prudence looked out of the window.

The house was shading the part of the yard where the vampire fell down. She had already gotten up and started climbing up the wall. Prudence tensed up, thinking about how she could even kill this thing when an arrow stuck in the vampire's body. Two more followed. Prudence could see that one found its target, and the vampire slid down the wall.

Prudence stood frozen, waiting for the vampire to move again. But there wasn’t anything except her own heartbeat and the sounds a dead body made. She looked down at her hand and yanked the fang out of it. Blood streamed down, washing the poison out of the wound.

“Is the crazy bitch gone?” Charlotte yelled. The sound made Prudence’s vision come back to normal. She ran to them, ignoring the pain in her body.

“I think she’s dead. How are…” Prudence stopped talking when she saw Charlotte crouching, her hand by her, trying to stifle Milo’s bleeding.

Milo was pale. Too pale. Prudence crouched over and focused on his heartbeat. Something wasn’t right.

“He’s not okay, is he?” Prudence’s voice was low. A low wail was stuck in her throat.

“We need to get him help. I need to get my phone and call Wentworth. Can ya stay with him?”

Prudence nodded and replaced Charlotte when she got up. Milo just then opened his eyes.

“You’re… hurt.”

Prudence looked at herself. Her whole body was covered in scratches, and there were several puncture wounds all around. She was certain one of her eyes was puffing up, and her face was stinging. Why was he worried about her? He can obviously feel the fact he is hurt worse. Prudence didn’t think that saying that would benefit anyone, so she focused on keeping him talking. "It's nothing; I can heal easily."

“I’m sorry you had to fight.” His voice was getting fainter. Prudence resisted the urge to hug him.

Prudence smiled at Milo. "I wanted to protect you guys.

You are important to me. And that is worth fighting for." As soon as the words exited her mouth, she realized they were true.

“Am I going to die?” Milo asked.

“No, we won’t let that happen. Charlotte would yell at death itself.” Prudence chuckled, trying to keep Milo’s hopes up. She sat there, hands pressed against Milo’s stomach and reassuring him he would be fine as a car pulled over, and someone ran in.

“Oh, my god, what happened?” Prudence heard Doctor Wentworth’s voice.

“Leave me alone, get Milo.”

Prudence avoided the doctor’s glance as he came in the hallway and administered first aid.

“He needs a hospital. Both of you do too.” The doctor tried to help Prudence with her wounds. She shifted away.

“I’ll be fine, take care of Charlotte and Milo.” Prudence got up, feeling faint. “They’re hurt worse, I’ll live.”

"Basement, casket-shaped fridge," Charlotte whispered when Prudence passed by.

Prudence walked into the basement and broke the lock on the fridge. She took out the blood and walked to the kitchen.

Milo had been busy writing down instructions and sticking them around the kitchen, so Prudence could do anything on her own. Prudence walked over to the oven and, after transferring the cold blood in a metal container, put it inside.

"It seems like a large microwave," she muttered to herself. Turning the dial, she waited for the blood to heat up to at least a drinkable temperature.

The pain had finally come to the forefront of her mind. Every wound on her body stung because of the sweat, and some of them oozed. It would have brought her to her knees if she wasn't so worried about Milo and Charlotte.

The blood heated up, and Prudence immediately drank as much of it as she could. She didn't pay attention to the taste, instead of forcing the hot liquid down her throat.

Her body had begun to heal up when her phone rang.

"Charlotte?"

"Both of us are okay." Charlotte hurried to reassure her. "They gave Milo a blood transfusion—"

"A what?"

"They gave him blood similar to the one in his body, but through a needle in his vein. It's a doctor thing."

"Oh." Prudence was surprised that they would do a procedure that reminded her of vampires that much.

"Then they fixed his wound. I got my arm set. What about ya?"

"I am drinking as much blood as I can. Healing slowly. I'll go outside later and try to figure out what to do with the vampire body."

“Burn it.” Charlotte’s voice was quiet. Prudence assumed it was because she was in public.

"Red can out in the back. Gasoline, the things we put in the car to make it run. Very flammable. Cover the thing in it, and then light a match. Don't get any on ya. Nothing can come back from that."

“Okay. When will you be back?”

“When they discharge us. Ya can come visit us when you get better and clean up.”

“I’d like that.”

* * *

THE DRY BLOOD came off so easily. Simple water and a towel, flowing down the drain. The oozing stopped right after I drank the blood. Wounds knit together, the new skin losing its pinkish hue almost immediately. I know this is not what happens in the hospital, but I can’t help but think of Milo’s transfusion. His fate might not lie in the balance, but I still feel like it is. I feel like it would break me if he died.

Blood heals wounds. It means life. It is what rushes through us like a river. I think back to when I emptied the veins of that poor woman in the ambulance. I will never forget that sound for as long as I live. It haunts me in my dreams, like the visions of death I have as my only memories.

Maybe that is the only thing that separates me from that

thing in the yard. Guilt. She didn't think about how she would feel after killing my friends or me. And I still sometimes wonder if the vampire hunter would have been something else if he grew up in a world where monsters like me don't exist. Maybe he would have raised a family. Instead, he spent his life causing pain.

Yes, I am a monster. Or I have a monster in me. I think I accepted that in the very moment I decided to fight back. The very moment I sunk my claws into the vampire's flesh. No amounts of showers and clothes will fix that. When I think of it, I feel numb but panicked at the same time.

How many people had she killed? How many people has she grinned at, while they crawl on the floor, trying to get away from her? Has she ever felt sad for the dying flames in someone's eyes? Was I like her?

That figure was looming above me in my nightmare. Was it a human or a vampire? I don't think I could tell. I didn't believe that cruelty like that existed. I thought that violence like the one I caused those innocent humans was a mark of something twisted inside me.

Maybe that defines us is our choices. Do we choose to protect others, or dismantle them? Do we fall down an abyss or rise up, refusing to give up? Charlotte walked into the grayness for me. Milo was apologizing to me on his deathbed. Why shouldn't I dive into my own gray for them? Even the thought of diving in and never resurfacing haunts the back of my thoughts.

I walk down the hall with the gasoline can with me. People said that fire was cleansing. Cleansing the soul. I think I have disagreed with that. At least now I do. It feels more like reducing something to something less. I don't mind reducing her.

The body in front of me is mangled and unnaturally twisted, the arrows protruding from it. Will I one day end up like this if the people who want me dead get their way? Pouring the gasoline over it and lighting the match, I am faced with more questions than answers.

In fact, I think I only have one answer.

The claws on my hands are weapons. They destroy. The fangs in my mouth are there for me to pray on things, on people. But whether or not I do that is my choice. I need to live with my decisions, and if I ever get reduced to the crackling, melting monstrosity I see before me, I need to die with peace of mind. Maybe then I'll stop being haunted by my decisions.

The ones hunting me are not right. They are like her. They choose destruction. They chose to come after me. They don't need to.

The need is hunger. Need is being afraid. Need is protecting the ones who care about you. Need is the only reason I will ever do anything like this. And I will live with my guilt. My ferocity doesn't control me.

As the flames flicker on, I make a promise. I will never be like her. But I will fight to live.

ABOUT THE AUTHOR

Dylan Keefer is a web designer / developer by day and a writer by night. He's basically a modern day superhero, using code and words to breathe creativity into reality. On a more serious note, he has been writing from a very young age and has always been pursuing the dream of writing professionally. Everything he does is in pursuit of that dream. He writes light-hearted as well as dark themed stories across multiple genres. His stories involve psychological struggles or moral dilemmas of the human condition. If you like those themes and the idea of questioning what it means to be human, then it won't matter what genre the story is; he will make you a believer.

Want Free Books?

Join my newsletter to receive updates on my new book releases go to my website at purplepress.org to sign up.

Join My Newsletter

Reviews are essential to my growth. If you enjoyed this book, I would love it if you took a moment to leave a honest review. A few sentences is plenty, just enough to let fellow readers know what you liked about this book.

Thank you in advance, we appreciate and couldn't do this without you.

For more information:
purplepress.org
PurplePressLLC@gmail.com

ALSO BY DYLAN KEEFER

Series

The Blood Rite Saga

The Blood Empire: Episode One

The Blood Princess: Episode One

The Blood Princess: Episode Two

The Blood Princess: Episode Three

The Blood Princess: Episode Four

The Chronicles of Gandos

The Sword of Light

The Aurora Chronicles

Child of Winter

Lake of Prophecy

Britney Allen: The London Crime Syndicate

Blood of Babes: The Slasher Files

Standalone

Lost in Space

The Lone Survivor

Mr. Buddy Bot

Evelyn

Printed in Great Britain
by Amazon

45003169R00099